red hats

also by damon wayans

Bootleg

red hats

a novel

DAMON WAYANS

ATRIA BOOKS

New York London Toronto Sydney

ATRIA BOOKS
A Division of Simon & Schuster, Inc.
1230 Avenue of the Americas
New York, NY 10020

This book is a work of fiction. Names, characters, places, and incidents either are products of the author's imagination or are used fictitiously. Any resemblance to actual events or locales or persons, living or dead, is entirely coincidental.

First Atria Books hardcover edition May 2010

ATRIA BOOKS and colophon are trademarks of Simon & Schuster, Inc.

For information about special discounts for bulk purchases, please contact Simon & Schuster Special Sales at 1-866-506-1949 or business@simonandschuster.com.

The Simon & Schuster Speakers Bureau can bring authors to your live event. For more information or to book an event, contact the Simon & Schuster Speakers Bureau at 1-866-248-3049 or visit our website at www.simonspeakers.com.

Designed by Suet Yee Chong

Manufactured in the United States of America.

10 9 8 7 6 5 4 3 2 1

Library of Congress Cataloging-in-Publication Data

Wayans, Damon.
Red hats : a novel / Damon Wayans.—1st Atria books hardcover ed.
p. cm.
1. African American women—Fiction. 2. Widows—Fiction.
3. Friendship—Fiction. I. Title.
PS3623.A953R43 2010
813'.6—dc22

2010004682

ISBN 978-1-4391-6461-7
ISBN 978-1-4391-6478-5 (ebook)

In life we all get a mother . . .
I just happened to get the most amazing one on the planet.
This book is dedicated to Elvira Wayans,
my inspiration.

When I am an old woman I shall wear purple
With a red hat which doesn't go, and doesn't suit me.

—JENNY JOSEPH

chapter one

The Boeing 767 began to shake like a carnival ride as the red seat-belt light flashed on. The captain put on his official intercom voice and told Alma what she already knew as a result of the water in her lap.

"Ladies and gentlemen, please remain in your seats and fasten your seat belts," the captain droned with authority. "I've been informed there's a severe weather system up ahead, and it may get a bit bumpy for a while."

"A bit?" Alma muttered as she fought to keep her stomach in the place God intended it to be. Right this minute, it was in her throat.

She peered out the tiny window to see a tar-black sky, blotted with angry, bruised clouds. Massive, blinding flashes of lightning, from beneath the rocking plane, convinced her they were doomed. Alma reached for Harold's hand. He was engrossed in the *New York Times* sports section and didn't even notice her trembling appendage.

"Harold!" she yelled.

"What, woman?" Harold fumed.

"We're goin' to crash." Alma started to weep.

"Woman, these things were made to withstand turbulence. Shut up and enjoy the ride." He laughed and went back to reading his paper.

Alma squinted her eyes, shooting tiny poisoned darts at him, knowing Harold would never take this tone with her had his feet been firmly on the ground. In a petulant fit, she grabbed the miniature bottle of whiskey he was sipping and sloshed the liquid at his face.

After twenty-seven years of marriage to this unpredictable woman, Harold had developed quick reflexes. The brown liquid splashed against the window as a flash of lightning lit the sky. The sticky liquor wandered slowly down the glass.

"What's wrong with you, Alma? Why do you always have to show out?" Harold demanded. "You can't just say, 'I'm scared'? You can't ask me nicely to hold your hand?"

"Why do I have to ask?" Alma tossed back.

Before it could get a firm hold, the coming argument was interrupted by a violent explosion in the rear of the plane. Alma joined the chorus of screams ripping through the now descending tube of death.

A bolt of lightning had hit the plane. The cabin began to fill with smoke. The plane jerked and sputtered. Alma could hear the engines shut off, and they began their stomach-clenching drop from the sky. *Shortly, I will return to these heavens. This time, though, I won't need to check no bags.* Alma prided herself on always being able to find some good in any situation.

The captain's breathless voice was heard again. He wasn't as cocky now. She could hear the tight knot in his throat as he warned them to assume crash position, which amounted to leaning forward as far as you were able so that, as Alma joked with Harold, "you can kiss your own ass good-bye!"

Harold smiled at her as the plane broke in half.

"'Bye, Alma," he called faintly as a deadly gust of wind and torrential rain jerked him from his seat, tossing him like an empty, worthless husk into the darkness below.

"No! Harold, don't leave me!" she begged. Alma attempted to loosen her seat belt to give a free-fall chase, but the latch wouldn't unlock. She pushed the call button for a stewardess—*ping ping ping.* Then, in the blink of an eye, she was falling, too. Alma gazed above to the somber sky as it distanced itself from her. She asked God to watch over Harold—*ping ping ping.*

Five twenty-seven A.M. Alma's eyes popped open. A strong will allowed her to force herself to wake up from the recurring nightmare, which included the two things she feared most in this world.

First, she dreamed she was flying in a plane, something she'd vowed she'd never do after witnessing firsthand the disaster of Flight 101 at Kennedy Airport. The plane was struck by lightning, fell from the sky, and burst into a fireball of death and lifelong pain for the families of the victims, some thirty years ago.

In her dream, sitting in the seat next to her was clueless Harold, her worthless husband.

She had no idea where they were going because money was scarce, always had been. Besides, there was absolutely no way in hell she'd willingly straddle that death cylinder. Not on her own, anyway. She shuddered, recalling the familiar climax to the nightmare.

With a violent, soaking thud, she slammed into the ocean waters, only to wish she had suffered a fatal heart attack and died, because in her sixty-four years, she'd never learned to swim—fear number two. She fought the giant waves as they crashed over her time and again.

Alma thought she'd never swallowed so much water in her entire life. She petitioned God either to help her or to take her life, because she couldn't breathe for another instant or drink another drop of this damn salty water.

Hallelujah! God was alive. The waters calmed. Alma used what little energy she had to roll over. She drifted weightlessly on her back as the blinding sun ordered the clouds away. Alma floated the distance to dry land but couldn't move. She lay in the hot sand, exhausted, allowing the even flow of the waves to rock her lovingly. Her eyelids became droopy.

Slowly, Alma stood, searching the area, calling for Harold, who was nowhere to be found. *How much time has passed?* She noticed a long row of footprints in the sand heading in the direction of a gathering of lazy, bending palms in the distance. She struggled to follow the footprints as they disappeared, one after another, beneath the zombielike shuffle of her sluggish walk. By the time Alma reached the trees, the clouds that had terrorized the dreary sky were gone.

The warmth of the sun calmed her nerves. As she passed the trees, Alma saw what looked like a paradise of exotic blossoms—gorgeous pinks and violets, yellows, purples and bright reds, a magnificent rainbow of colors—rising from a meticulously manicured island of lush green grass, giving over to reed and towering brown and tan cattails.

"Isn't this the living end, Harold?" she asked, searching for his hand. It took her a moment to remember he wasn't with her any longer.

"Alma, help me!" Harold's voice shouted, seemingly from nowhere. She turned to see him in the distance, fighting to stay above the same waves she had battled, to escape the powerful pull of the ocean's hungry maw.

Alma pumped her arms from side to side to propel herself to Harold's aid. But her legs didn't move. She looked down to see she was covered to the knees in quicksand. As she attempted to break free of its wet grip, the loose sand swallowed her further downward.

"God, please help me! I can't go through this hell again!" Alma cried. "Not another time!" The sand recognized her attempt to escape and pulled her further into its gritty embrace. God was not listening this time.

Up to her neck and sure to smother, Alma looked at the ocean for a final glimpse of Harold before he surrendered to his own demise. Alma closed her bloodshot eyes and whispered a hollow *I'm sorry* to Harold, to God, then to herself. She took one long breath and disappeared into the deep.

Waking was the last thing Alma expected, and breathing never felt sweeter. Having the nightmare for the third time that week put her in a sour mood. She nudged Harold, who was lying next to her in the bed, to make certain he wasn't truly dead. It was more like a little kick, but it worked. Harold rolled over.

"Harold, are you all right?" Alma asked.

"Yeah, I'm all right! What's wrong with you, woman? I'm trying to sleep here," he whined.

Alma lay still, pretending to be asleep. She must have overnudged him. Harold sucked his teeth greedily and went back to sleep. When he began snoring, Alma reached for her Zoloft on the night table next to her half-glass of room-temperature water that helped the nasty-tasting pills get past her gag reflex.

Mumbling her disdain at the only thing that kept her from being labeled everything from a classic nut job to a psycho slasher, she got up to begin her day. Getting out of bed had become a chore of late, as she'd put on a few extra pounds—sixteen extra, to be exact. Alma's physician said weight gain was a side effect of the drugs he prescribed to combat the "change." Other side effects included dry mouth, headache, dizziness, drowsiness, nausea, vomiting, constipation, fainting, blurred vision, and the possibility of an irregular heartbeat. Alma had told pudgy Dr. Know-it-all Simms the drugs would do her in quicker than the menopause. He laughed. She didn't.

Alma gazed into the mirror but didn't like what she saw. Her change of life was truly life-changing. *Hah!* Steel-gray hairs were beginning to show again at the roots. It hadn't been two weeks since her last coloring. *What's happening to me?*

Alma splashed cool water on her face and washed the crusty sleep from the corners of her eyes, her most expressive feature. It seemed only yesterday she was staring at the red circle on the calendar marking her twenty-first birthday. Now that same red mark was a cold reminder that sixty-five was charging like a freight train and would arrive in three short weeks. Alma wasn't looking forward to being a government-certified senior citizen.

She turned on the digital radio, the one Harold recently bought her, to the oldies station, made a pot of Folgers, and toasted four pieces of white bread—two light and two dark. She'd eat the two light slices, and Harold would have the others. Alma had stopped cooking a real and healthy breakfast for him ages ago, because he'd stopped saying thank you after every meal. Even worse, he never asked why she'd stopped. In fact, Alma couldn't remember the last time she'd done anything nice for the man. She often referred to him as her *has-been* rather than her *husband.* She thought it was funny. Harold said it was cruel but absolutely refused to admit it hurt his feelings, knowing that was exactly what she meant to do.

To make matters worse, Alma didn't read the morning paper because she was interested in anything it offered, she did it simply to piss Harold off. He hated anybody to read the paper before he did. It was a pet peeve. Alma accidentally dropped a bit of strawberry jelly on the front page of the sports section and wiped it across the headline in an attempt to clean it off. She folded the paper neatly and positioned it facedown in front of Harold's place setting.

The smell of Folgers never failed to wake Harold up. It made his mouth water and got him to drag his lazy butt downstairs. Once he smelled it, he had to have some.

Their eyes locked as he strolled into the kitchen, fully dressed.

"Good morning," he offered without conviction.

"What's so damn good about it?" Alma shot back. "I

couldn't sleep a gnat of a second because you was snoring again like a damn polar bear. Then you went and took all the covers off me in the middle of the night."

"Maybe I was trying to get me some of that sweet stuff you keep locked up under all them covers," he said with a lewd wink. "You know a man's got needs, Alma."

"I told you I ain't giving you nothing 'til you start acting right. You've gotta earn this, honey," she teased, using her best Mae West.

"How can I do that?" Harold said as he walked to where she was sitting and made an attempt to kiss the back of her neck. Alma pushed him away.

"Don't do that! If I want your lousy kisses, I'll ask for them."

Harold sucked his teeth and headed for the stove, angry at himself for allowing her to sucker him, yet another stab to his already ailing heart. He poured himself a cup of coffee and sat in his seat at the head of the pale green, rickety table. At least she hadn't taken this from him. His position at the head of the table was the last bit of power Harold had left in this house. He made a mental note never to tell her how important that station was to him, because she'd surely confiscate his God-given right to a man's throne.

The silence spoke volumes. Years of resentment had festered to the point of this hurtful, cancerous relationship. Harold avoided conversation with Alma because he knew it always ended in an argument or a fight. He decorated his coffee with four lumps of sugar and a tiny dollop of cream. Drank it dark and sweet, just like his woman used to be.

Harold ate a piece of toast to line his stomach before popping his heart pills. He hated the chalky taste they left in his mouth and took a generous swig of Jack Daniel's from the flask his mother had given him for his tenth wedding anniversary.

You're going to need this to get you through the next ten years of this marriage, son, the card had read. *God help you.*

Harold kept the card hidden in a battered shoebox in the back of the closet, knowing Alma wouldn't get his mother's brand of humor—too much truth to it. She'd only try to retaliate with her own brand. He should have lit the card and tossed it into the garbage years ago, because Alma knew every nook and cranny of the apartment.

"God help you, too, you old bat," Alma had said the day she found the card.

Harold lifted the newspaper, immediately reacting to the sticky jelly on his hand.

"Did you do this to my paper, woman?"

"Do what?" Alma asked sweetly.

Harold sucked his teeth, mad at himself for asking the obvious. One point for her, he thought.

"I had another bad dream last night," Alma blurted out.

"Oh?" Harold challenged.

"Yeah, we were on a plane and . . ."

"It crashed, right into the ocean," Harold spewed, cutting her off. "You told me that one twice already. It's the medicine that's giving you them dreams, Alma. Ask the doctor to change your dosage." She went stiff at his dismissal.

Harold returned to the sports section. The sounds of Marvin Gaye singing "Mercy, Mercy Me" on the radio calmed his nerves. He poured a little more whiskey into his cup, then sat, sipped his brew, and avoided Alma's gaze.

"You keep on drinking that Jack Daniel's, and you're going to burn the liver right out of your side," she warned.

Harold waved her off again, this time with a heavy sigh. He couldn't wait for the buzz to kick in and obliterate her piercing stare and harping voice. It gave him the heebie-jeebies.

"What time will you be home?" Alma asked.

"I don't know," Harold mumbled sheepishly.

"You can't answer me?"

"I said I don't know!" he shouted.

"You say it like a retarded kid on a yellow school bus. If I was that whore Rae Ann across the street, you sure could open your mouth and speak."

"Don't start, Alma. It's too early for this." Harold winced.

"So, when is a good time, because we need to talk?"

"What's your schedule like in 2020?"

One point for me. Harold was proud of his response. The alcohol must have kicked in, because he felt warm inside, unafraid of the woman whose squinty eyes shot daggers in his direction. Besides, he loved her too much to run from her. Years of Alma's verbal abuse had forced Harold to sharpen his wits.

"I hope to be at your God damned funeral way before 2020, you ugly bastard," Alma spat back at him. Her eyes were now like slits. Once they disappeared under her lids, it meant she was mad as hell and sure to be on the attack.

That was Harold's cue to leave. He had pushed the wrong button now, and bad things were about to happen. He wished he'd kept his mouth shut. Alma picked up her coffee and threw it in his face. He felt lucky it was cold from sitting.

He wiped his face and headed for the front door. Alma rushed to the door and caught it before it closed. Harold looked up at her from halfway down the first flight of the steep, narrow steps.

"I hate you! I hope you fall down the rest of those stairs and break your neck!" Alma screamed. As if she had all the time in the world, she turned and stepped into the darkness of the apartment.

How could she say such hurtful things? Harold carefully held the railing as he made his way cautiously down the four remaining flights of steps. He didn't want to give Alma the satisfaction of his falling. That would make it two points for her.

chapter two

The Zoloft began to take effect while Alma watched Harold quicken his pace as he exited their building. She decided against throwing a flowerpot or a skillet—anything would do—down at him, courtesy of the drugs. Instead, she reflected on how much she had loved that man for what now seemed like eons. Alma hated where their relationship had ended up. They were once the envy of the neighbors, holding hands and practically skipping down the street.

While they didn't have lots of money, they had made up for it with an abundance of love. His kisses were treats then and tasted like See's candy. Those kisses kept her waiting for her Harold to return home from his job at the Check Cash. Back then, before he had to add a second job, they would stay up all night laughing, talking, and making love.

She couldn't understand how he simply could not talk to her, not about anything real. She had to pick fights just to get him to speak. It had been almost five years of the silent treatment. A husband should share things with his wife. She wondered if he was still mad because she hadn't let his mother in the house. Was it her fault he wasn't home and she didn't trust strangers in her home? A nosy stranger was exactly what that woman was to her.

From the get-go, Alma and Beatrice had hated each other. Beatrice had raised Harold to be a momma's boy. Whatever his momma needed his momma got. Then Alma walked into his life, and Harold turned his heart away from the only woman he had been led to believe he could ever love. Momma.

It was the dead of winter, and she'd decided simply to drop by. Didn't she own a phone? She knew where Harold worked, but Alma felt she wanted to come in and criticize the way she kept house. Nothing Alma did had ever been good enough.

"Harold likes his clothes washed in Downy. Put a strip of Bounce in the dryer to get rid of the static cling," Beatrice would scold. "Harold doesn't like his chicken baked. Where are all the pictures of his family?"

In the beginning, Alma had tried to accommodate her. She hung more family photos, changed her laundry detergent, and even learned Beatrice's famous chicken cacciatore recipe. It wasn't enough. Nothing she ever did was good enough for Beatrice's little Harold, so Alma decided to push back. She'd zero in and criticize Beatrice's weight.

"Why does it take you so long to get up these stairs, Bee? Why do you wear those run-over shoes, Bee? Why do you wear that perfume that smells like a two-dollar hooker, Bee?" She called her Bee because it was short for the *bitch* that she was.

That particular day, Bee had popped by in a snow storm, ringing the buzzer like a madwoman. Alma knew who it was, because she saw the fat blimp covered in snow from the window of her cozy apartment. She made up her mind that very day to draw a line in the snow.

Beatrice is Harold's mother and not mine, Alma had reminded herself as she cranked up the music to drown out the constant buzz from the intercom. Alma smiled as she watched the porker looking up at her, waving those stubby little arms to get her attention. Their eyes met before Alma closed the blinds.

Harold had later blamed her for his mother's pneumonia and resulting death. Alma had refused to accept the blame, saying, "God doesn't love ugly, and fat-ugly is what Beatrice was."

Precious Momma was barely laid out before the town whore, Rae Ann Steele, had Harold running across the street at her beck and call. God, she hated that woman like the flu! Having no man of her own, Rae Ann was free to seduce every man, married or not, in the neighborhood. They paid her rent and bought her booze for the few minutes of pleasure she could provide. Alma had caught her several times dancing naked in her window, trying to get Harold's attention.

"Why do you want to see that *National Geographic* strip show?" Alma had asked Harold.

"At least she's putting out," Harold had replied. He was referring to the fact that he and Alma hadn't had sex in about three years. She got tired of him hanging out with his friends until two in the morning, then creeping into her bed, pulling her panties to the side without even a kiss or an *I missed you, baby* before the quickest of quickies ever perpetrated. Determined not to be an enabler of bad sex, Alma had told him he was cut off. She would hit him if he tried to touch her again.

"Sex with me is a privilege," she had declared. To make sure he kept his unwanted *thing* out of her, she would constantly remind him that he wasn't a good lover. He was undesirable to her.

Looking out the window was Alma's favorite pastime. It seemed as if everyone led an exciting life but her. The place was too quiet since the kids had left home. She couldn't understand why they didn't visit more often despite her pleas. After all, she was getting old and wouldn't be around much longer. Her mother had died at the age of seventy-two from what they called natural causes. Alma didn't think there was anything natural about death.

Why would God put eternity into our hearts and then let us get old and die? It just didn't seem right. Alma was at the age when death comes calling. The thing about death is that it doesn't discriminate. Death is greedy for life—young or old, black or white, rich or poor, and even the unborn, her mother used to tell her. It ain't happy unless it gets three in a row, according to the old wives' tale. Lately, Alma wished it would call her number so she could stop wondering *when*.

With the kids off riding the ups and down of their own roller coasters, Alma felt death would satisfy her excuse for being so lonely. She knew part of the reason her children stayed away was that they didn't like to hear the truth. Alma prided herself on being honest. Even if you didn't ask, she was going to tell you what she thought, about anything and everything. For instance, she had told her daughter, Angel, that her ex-football-player husband, Darryl, wasn't worth a damn.

"Momma, I love him," Angel had explained.

"Ain't that much love in the whole world, baby. He don't treat you right. He's lazy and beneath you. Whatever happened to that nice boy, Randy Stanton, you used to like?"

"He's dead. Got shot robbing a liquor store ten years ago, Momma."

"What about Terrance?"

"T-Bone? Please, Momma. Look, I know you don't like Darryl, but I made a commitment to him before God to honor my marriage. I'm not going to leave him because you don't like him. Now, I would appreciate if you would just try to get along with him when he is around."

"OK. If you want to put *that* before your mother, go right ahead, but I can't be phony. I got a feeling about him. You'll see."

Darryl had signed a big contract with a professional football team, and as soon as they got married, the chubby faked an injury the first year he played. They bought him out of the contract for a fraction of its worth. The fool thought he would get picked up by another team he really wanted to play for, but that didn't happen, because they found out the injury was bogus. The first team sued him, and he had to pay the money back.

Now he ate like a football player on a security guard's salary. He was fat and bitter and took it out on poor Angel. Once he was stupid enough to hit Angel in front of Alma. She had pulled a butcher knife on him and threatened to kill him if he ever put his meaty hands on her baby again. Just to make sure he knew she wasn't playing, Alma had given him a little cut on the fleshy part of his right cheek, something to remember her by. Six stitches later, he had packed them up and moved them to Texas. He'd said it was because the land was cheaper than in New York, but she knew it was because he had seen his life flash before his fat, bulging eyes.

Sometimes Alma regretted what she'd done, because it cost her a relationship with her granddaughter, Nia. Alma loved the ground that baby crawled on. There was nothing more beautiful to her in the world. Alma looked forward to the summers when Angel would come visit her for a couple of weeks, where she got a chance to play Grandma with Nia. *Grandma!* She was repulsed by the word. Thank God, Nia was so adorable when she said "Gan-ma" that it didn't have the same sting as when she heard it correctly in her head.

Her younger son, twenty-two-year-old Jesse, was a so-called musician. A bum and a pothead was more along the lines of what Alma thought. Jesse would come by her house stinking like cheap booze and that musky marijuana odor mingled with sweat. It made her want to retch. He'd be so high that as soon as he sat down or leaned against something for support, he'd nod off.

"What kind of fun is that high?" she had asked him.

"It makes me creative," he'd replied.

"It needs to make you employed," Alma had snapped as she dug in her pocketbook for spare change, a ritual during Jesse's inebriated visits.

"I need more than ten dollars. I'm trying to buy this new horn. It's beautiful. Wynton Marsalis says this trumpet is made from the god of music. Please, Momma, it will take my skills to the next level," Jesse had begged.

"Don't try to con me. Ten dollars is all you're going to get, and if you keep bugging me, I will take that back. God don't love no junkies, boy. You're a sinner in the Lord's eyes."

"You messing up my high, Momma," Jesse had offered

in his defense. He'd eventually stopped coming by, probably because Alma constantly reminded him of his spiritually disapproved state.

Two semesters shy of a bachelor's degree in communications, and he'd decided music was his calling. But Coltrane he was not.

"Just because you can make a horn squawk don't mean you can play it," she had said to him.

"You never even heard me play before. You're a dream killer, Momma."

"And you're a mother killer, because you dropped out of college."

Jesse was her problem child. He had issues Alma knew only God could heal. To compensate, she gave him a little money now and then to keep him from getting desperate or criminal.

Her older son, Todd, was her pride and joy. He had turned out as well as a mother could hope for, except for the white woman he married. Alma was jealous of the lavish wedding he'd had with Helga. It was the kind of ceremony she'd always told Todd she dreamed of having.

"Why'd you want to marry that?" she had asked him.

"Because I love her, Momma. She's a great mother to my children, always positive and loving, plus she supports my goals. We're a team, just like the good Lord intended," Todd had explained.

"All that sounds good, son, but don't they make them like that in a black?" Alma had asked sarcastically.

"Momma, could you please be happy because I'm happy?"

"I don't see how you can love the oppressor of your people."

"She's German."

"Well, it's like the Jews were black and they oppressed them. Same thing."

"Momma!"

"OK, I will keep my thoughts to myself. If you love your little wet dog, I'll try to still love you."

Todd was an architect for a large firm in Germany. That's where he had met the white girl, Helga. All in all, Alma couldn't complain too much about Todd, because he took care of his mother. He had put her on a defined-benefits plan that gave her a monthly check for a couple grand. With Harold's Social Security check and his pension plan, they did just fine for themselves.

Todd had two children, or *mutts* as she saw them. Their names were Hansel and Gretel, a horrid idea the white woman came up with. She thought it might be fun for them as they grew up. School would be hell for them. Alma was offended that the names she'd picked, Draden and Mikyla, were not even considered. In protest, Alma wouldn't call them by their given names. Instead, she called them "children" or "kids." Alma had only seen pictures of them, although she had spoken with them on the phone. They sounded funny to her ears. German accents just didn't sound right coming out of the mouths of little black faces.

Even if she couldn't actually see them, the very idea bothered her.

Alma closed her eyes and swayed to the sounds of Sam Cooke singing "When I Fall in Love." The lyrics reminded her of her teenage years, sneaking into the Apollo to see Jackie Wilson with her best girlfriend, Donna. The security guards would harass them for their phone numbers and threaten to turn them away if they didn't oblige, but since Alma was so fine, they'd let her stand in the wings watching Jackie make the girls in the audience swoon.

Jackie once tried hitting on Alma until he found out she was only fourteen years old. Though the relationship was deferred, it was enough to make her a legend among her friends. They were jealous. Donna and the rest of the girls couldn't for the life of them understand why she told Jackie her real age.

"If you lie to a man in the beginning of your relationship, you will have to lie throughout," Alma told them.

The song reminded her of the good times between Harold and herself. Alma smiled at the thought of the first time she had met Harold, at the Savoy Club. When he walked into the smoke-filled room, he literally took her breath away. Alma recalled him floating toward her, wearing a smile that said, *Excuse me, miss, may I spend eternity with you?* He was so handsome it made Alma's knees weak. Had he not taken her hand and asked her to dance, she was sure the floor would have been the next thing she felt.

Harold had been dressed to kill in a beige pin-striped linen suit with a crisp white shirt and burgundy tie. He looked brand new, as if God had just made him. And that man could dance his ass off! They boogied all night to long songs, fast songs, slow songs, and in-between songs. They even danced to the a cappella songs, because their bodies had their own rhythm. A woman could tell a lot about a man by the way he moved on a dance floor. Alma had learned enough to know that the chemistry they created in that crowded dance hall would only intensify if they were alone in a candlelit bedroom.

Shortly after their encounter, despite Alma's strict Christian upbringing, her flesh had betrayed her heart, despite her mind saying, *This is wrong, and God will judge you if you lie with this man.* Like Eve, who defiantly ate the fruit from the Tree of Knowledge, Alma lay with him. She didn't feel the immediate effects of her sin, and she continued to give herself to this man who consumed and devoured every part of her. Harold touched and kissed areas she didn't know she had. He was a slow, gentle lover, with patience and a true desire to please a willing virgin.

For three months straight, every day except the ones forbidden by nature, they had made exquisite love. Eventually, like Eve in the garden, Alma had begun to feel the effects of her sin. Telling her mother she was pregnant was the toughest conversation she'd ever have. It was also the shortest conversation, cut off by the front door opening and Alma being ushered out of her devout Christian home before God's wrath sent fire from the heavens to destroy them all.

Alma had nowhere to go except back to the arms of her lover, who gladly welcomed her and quickly married her to provide his queen the dignity she deserved. Alma was disappointed in the way they got married. It wasn't romantic at all. He didn't get down on one knee—he didn't even formally propose. They had simply gone downtown and got married in street clothes. Not the way she'd fantasized about getting hitched at all. There was supposed to be music playing, with family and friends gathered in celebration against a scenic background. Not a small room void of any flowers or wedding decorations, with a stranger as a witness to their lifelong union. Sometimes Alma wondered if the coldness of their wedding had to do with the coldness of their marriage. Todd had barely been one year old when she found out she was pregnant with Angel. Eighteen months after Angel, she and Harold had had a sit-down.

"I'm pregnant again."

"How'd you do that?" Harold had asked. "We haven't been doing nothing regular for a while now."

"It only takes one time," Alma had stated.

"I think you should get your tubes tied. We can't afford no more kids."

"I think *you* should get *your* tubes tied. I've already sacrificed my body giving birth," she'd replied.

"Alma, they can tie you up in the delivery room. It's

simple. Everything is already opened up. I don't see the problem with you doing it."

"The problem is, I may still want some more children. Just because you say we can't afford them don't mean I don't want them."

"Fine! I'll get a vasectomy," he'd shouted.

After the operation, Harold wasn't the same. He said he felt less than a man. She told him it was all in his head, but he did have a hard time getting it up for her after the vasectomy. Alma had felt bad for him. Maybe she shouldn't have pushed him to do it. Maybe things would be a lot different.

Now, between the music and her trip down memory lane, Alma made up her mind to cook for Harold tonight. Perhaps they could have a decent conversation for a change, instead of arguing all the time. It would be nice to reminisce with him. She would even make some of his favorite, peach cobbler. If he was really nice, she would give her has-been a piece of herself for dessert.

chapter three

Harold sat across from his childhood friend, Bob, studying the chess pieces before him. Bob was like a junkyard dog with shaggy black hair, always a bit unkempt. He never strayed too far from the neighborhood. He was a divorced veteran and father of eight children, who had fought and won several battles with prostate cancer. He turned his attention to the coffee stains on Harold's shirt. The third musketeer, their buddy Seymour, observed their moves from the sidelines.

"What happened to you? Scare a flock of pigeons on your way here?" Bob joked.

"No, only Alma. She was feeling feisty this morning."

"Again?"

"Yeah, she got mad and threw her coffee on me," Harold said.

"You need to leave that crazy woman," Seymour offered.

"For who, and exactly where would I go? She ain't that bad. She's just an acquired taste, that's all. Going through that female transition is hard on her. She needs me."

"For what? To abuse?" Bob replied.

"It's OK. I can take it. She loves me—just don't know how to show it. That's marriage. See, I understand what I signed up for. Most people don't."

"What'd you sign up for?" Bob was determined to not let up.

"I signed up for God's view of commitment. Till death do us part."

"She's gonna kill you, all right," Seymour stated.

"Nah. Alma has a good heart. I've seen this woman sacrifice for my family. When things got bad, she stepped up, went to work and helped take care of the bills, and still came home, made dinner, and put the kids to bed. She didn't complain or try to make me feel bad. She just rolled up her sleeves and did what she had to do. I have to love that woman."

"Well, she scares the bejesus out of me," Bob said.

"Me too," Seymour confessed. Seymour was a good-looking man. He had hazel eyes and wavy hair the young girls always wanted to braid and play with. Alcohol had bloated his once athletic body, and the constant squinting from his cigarette smoke make his Smokey Robinson eyes leak. He kept a napkin in hand to dab at the moist corners of his eyes. "That's why I'm never getting married," he said while dabbing.

"You ain't getting married because no one wants your infirm behind," Harold kidded.

"Look who's talking about infirm, Mr. Heart Problems. I'm gonna call you the Tin Man. You better go to the Wizard and ask him for a new ticker."

"I'll ask him for some eye drops for you while I'm there," Harold fired back.

"Good one," Bob stated. Playing the dozens was part of the joy of their friendship. Almost nothing was sacred with them.

Back in the day, Seymour, Bob, and Harold used to be a singing group, before the realities of life kicked in and they came to understand that doo-wop wasn't going to pay their bills. They called themselves Sweet Love. Their height of fame came on the street corners, where young girls would scream their names. Today, they still got accolades and sexual advances from the more mature women who remembered the sweet sounds of Sweet Love.

Harold was the lead singer and choreographer of their moves. He loved to dance and could still cut a rug with the best. He had picked up tickets to the Renaissance Ballroom to celebrate Alma's birthday in a few weeks. He was going to surprise her with dinner, dancing, and a beautiful bouquet of pink roses and bird-of-paradise—a little of the traditional with something exotic—delivered to the house. These were Alma's favorites. The day was designed to make her receptive to the rest of the niceties he had planned for the evening. He was hoping that if he did something as sweet and romantic as devoting an entire day to the celebration of his wife, perhaps she would let him have some peace for a couple of hours in return. Maybe.

Alma was so unpredictable, especially as she was getting older. Between the change of life and the various mood-altering medications, he never knew which Alma he was going to return home to or wake up next to. Sometimes she would be happy and so funny he couldn't get enough of her. That particular woman had a laugh that lit up a room. It was infectious. When she laughed, he laughed. He guessed that was one of the things that kept him hanging in there with her. Her laugh! Too bad she was so stingy with it.

"Your move," Bob said.

"Oh, I'm sorry. Woolgathering, I guess," Harold replied absentmindedly. He maneuvered his pawn to take Bob's bishop.

"What were you thinking about? The time Alma chased Seymour with that butcher knife?" Bob teased.

"Nah, I try to forget that," Harold said.

"Me too," Seymour added.

"That was funny. I've never seen a man run so fast. She was going to kill you."

"She was going to kill you, too, as I remember," Harold said.

"She sure was, told me to give this stab wound to you. I thought she was playing around until she swung that big ol' butcher knife at my face," Bob said. "I ran like hell."

Harold took out a fifth of whiskey and three small plastic cups from a brown paper bag and placed them on the stone table.

"I was wondering when you was going to bring out that kryptonite," Bob said as he helped himself to a generous shot of the warm, amber hooch.

"Mmmm, that's good stuff right there. You want some, Seymour?" Bob asked.

"Yeah, pass it this way," Seymour said. "Yep. That's the joy of life right there. You want me to pour you some more, Harold?"

Harold was holding his head in his hands. He pushed the cup away as if it was the source of his pain.

"No. My head is hurting."

"She hit you in the head, too?" Seymour joked.

"No. I've just been feeling funny the past few days. It's like I don't have all my energy. I just want to sleep, that's all. Even when I'm sleeping, I don't feel rested," he tried to explain.

"Maybe you should see a doctor," Bob suggested.

"See a doctor for what? The doctor is the one that got me on all these pills. Them people only think about one thing when you walk in the hospital, and it ain't you. It's how much insurance you got. They determine how much money they can get before they tell you what you got. If your insurance is real good, they give you cancer. They make a killing if they give you cancer. Between the chemo and the blood transfusions, along with the needles and tests, plus the cost of the room, that's over a hundred thousand dollars from one person. I don't want to know what I got anymore. When the good Lord wants me, he will come and get me. No doctor is going to stop that!"

"Amen," Bob said as he poured himself another shot.

"Y'all finish the rest of that. I'm going home to rest. I feel tired." Harold got up to leave.

"OK, but I won by forfeit," Bob said.

Harold nodded defeat.

From the living-room window, Alma looked in the direction of the park, hoping to see Harold. She couldn't for the life of her figure out why he spent so much time with Mutt and Jeff. Why couldn't he devote some time to the so-called love of his life? From sunup until sundown, he was in that park. All they did was sit there, drink, and play chess. What was so much fun about that? Wasn't she fun to him anymore?

Her mind drifted back to a hot summer's day when they'd gone on an overnight getaway to Virginia Beach. She and Harold went swimming late at night in the hotel's pool, which was supposed to be off limits after ten P.M. Adventure got the best of them, along with some Boone's Farm, and they had found themselves in the pool. They were wearing their street clothes when the notion struck, so they swam in their underwear.

The water was warm, and it had aroused Alma with the thrill of breaking the rules with this beautiful man and his lean, muscular frame, who kept kissing the tender spot at the nape of her neck. That was the first time she made love in a pool. She couldn't tell which wetness was hers and which was the pool's as Harold moved inside her. Once they had defiled the pool, they began to dry off, using the hotel towels stacked near the lounge chairs.

Harold had taken his underwear off and wrapped a towel around his waist. As they were walking toward their hotel room, Alma snatched the towel from Harold's waist and ran. She knocked loudly on every door she passed while Harold gave chase. They barely made it inside the room without being seen by patrons who opened their doors to see what the commotion was all about. Laughs like that had been the norm for them then. *Where did the spontaneity go? I'd give anything for us to laugh like that again.*

Now, at the window, Alma caught sight of Harold stumbling toward the building. *That's why I don't like him hanging around those good-for-nothings in the park.* Harold almost collided with a small group of women, each wearing a red hat. The shades varied from a ruby red to light pink, including everything in between. Each hat was styled differently. They looked like a group of churchgoers, only this was a Monday evening. The ladies gracefully avoided Harold's wobbly walk.

"All that drinking is going to kill you, old man," Alma scolded as Harold teetered into the apartment. "You look like one of the neighborhood bums, with your clothes all wrinkled and your eyes rolled back in your head like a crazy man. But don't pay me no mind. You just keep on doing what you want to do. It's your life you're throwing away."

Harold grumbled. Alma noticed he was sweating more than usual. Harold fumbled with his jacket, trying to hang it in the hallway closet. The jacket fell to the floor. He seemed too tired to bend over and pick it up and kicked a crumpled sleeve inside the closet and shut the door.

Alma was surprised that he didn't make a fuss over the wonderful aroma of her peach cobbler. She had spent the day making fried chicken, macaroni and cheese, yams, and collard greens. Topping it off was her famous peach cobbler. Why didn't he dance his way over to the stove and tell her how much he missed her cooking? Instead, Harold offered her a weak smile, then used the wall as a guide to the bedroom.

"I cooked for you," Alma said, a little sweeter than she'd like to have sounded.

"Thank you, baby, but I just need to lie down right now. My head's about to explode. I'll have a plate when I wake up," he said weakly. His steps were halting and uneven. Harold made it to the bed and allowed his body to fall face-forward into his feather pillow. Alma was pissed.

What an ungrateful man. I should throw all that good

food in the garbage just to teach him a lesson. He didn't even notice how good I look. Bastard didn't even look at me.

"I hope you die in your sleep, old man," she whispered to herself.

An hour slid by, and Alma got tired of waiting for Harold to wake up. After forty-five minutes, she gave up on the hope of sharing a candlelit dinner. Maybe something was wrong. Cooking had made her hungry, so she began taking little pinches of food. First a small piece of chicken breast and then just a tablespoon of macaroni and cheese followed by a tiny slice of yams. After sampling everything, she told herself Harold didn't know what he was missing, and she went ahead and ate a big plate with plenty of everything. That would show him.

It's not like him to sleep this long, Alma worried. Taking naps was normal for Harold, but he power-napped, forty minutes maximum. Alma had given him a little extra time, but now enough was enough. She didn't cook all that food for nothing. Alma marched into the bedroom.

"Harold Steven Washington, get your ass out of that bed and come eat this food before I throw it on you!" she yelled.

Harold was silent. She wondered why he was lying so still. She thought it must be hard to breathe with his face buried in the pillow like that. Alma moved to the bed and gave him a shake.

"Harold, wake up! Wake up, damn it!"

She turned him over. His face was blue. She touched his forehead, and his skin felt clammy.

"Harold? Oh, God! Harold! Wake up!" Alma cried.

Harold was dead, and she knew it. He wasn't breathing. His eyes weren't moving the way they did when she checked some nights.

"Harold, please wake up. I'm sorry! I won't talk to you like that anymore. Please wake up, Harold. Don't leave me. Please don't leave me! I'm so sorry. I promise I'll be a better wife!"

Alma climbed onto the bed, next to him, and cried.

chapter four

The week leading up to the funeral had been the longest of Alma's life. Waiting for the autopsy results was almost as emotionally draining as finding Harold's lifeless body. Coronary thrombosis was the verdict, due to arrhythmias. A heart attack, go figure!

Why did this have to fall on me? It's hard enough to lose someone you love, then there's the funeral arrangements, picking out a coffin, and, worst of all, calling family and friends to relate the bad news. She felt most people were thinking, *Good for you, Alma, serves you right!* They wanted to see her suffer. That's why they all showed up, to see her in misery.

In the pews behind her, she could hear whispering. She couldn't make out exactly what they were saying, but the snippets that did slip through stabbed her already broken heart.

"I'm surprised he lasted this long, all she put him through," a woman whispered too loudly behind her.

Angel held her hand tightly enough to restrain Alma from turning around and spitting fire at her accuser. Alma was grateful to have her daughter by her side to get her through all the pain.

"Your daddy is gone," she had sobbed into the phone. On the other end of the line, she could hear what sounded like a wounded animal caught in a steel trap.

Angel put Alma before her own feelings of loss, and Alma was thankful. She had jumped on the next plane to come be with her momma. She had always been a daddy's girl, so helping her mother do all the things you have to do for the dead was a way of expressing devotion to the man who loved, chastised, and validated her. Through her tears, Angel had found time to cook an assorted spread for the reception that would follow the funeral. It reminded Alma of the last meal she had cooked for Harold. She hoped never to see another macaroni and cheese in her life!

Bob and Seymour had spread the news that Sweet Love was officially over—their best friend was gone. Alma had slept in the living room, not wanting to enter the bedroom again. Angel had taken her to the doctor for more antianxiety medication, fearing her mother was on the precipice of a nervous breakdown. Alma wished the drugs the doctor gave her were stronger. She wanted to drown out the voice in her head that had wished Harold would die in his sleep.

She wanted to be numb like Jesse, who sat in the front row with a stupid look on his face from the reefers or whatever else he smoked. She had almost asked him to light her up a joint so she could justify exactly how surreal this situation was. Lord knew she didn't have any more tears to cry. She wondered where this reserve of salt water had come from. Was it the slide show on her wall of memories, she and Harold playing against their favorite songs? Songs like "Call Me" by Aretha Franklin, Al Green's "Let's Stay Together," and "When a Man Loves a Woman." Gotta love Percy Sledge. This was the song Harold had dedicated to Alma after their first big fight twenty-something years ago.

The fight had happened right after Todd was born. Harold kept complaining the baby was stinking. They both smelled it, but the source of the funk couldn't be found. After changing his diaper several times, wiping every crack and crevice in his wrinkled little behind, Alma became irritated at Harold's accusations of her being an unfit mother. She snapped and slammed doors, broke lots of little things—the pink candy dish that had been a wedding gift, a saucer here and a bowl there from the family china set—bits and pieces to help soothe her frustration.

"I can't find the stink! I put him in the tub and washed

everything, everywhere. Maybe he's sick," she had reasoned.

"Did you wash under his neck?" Harold had asked.

"What do you mean? He don't have no neck," Alma had replied.

Harold had lifted Todd's tiny head and pulled back the skin, revealing a crease filled with stinky baby cheese that made them both bend at the middle and gag. It took a few days to eliminate the odor completely. After that incident, Alma had made it a point to wash Todd's neck every time she changed his diaper. Todd had the cleanest neck in baby history.

Now the preacher finished earning his money, sending Harold to heaven. Alma was ready to leave, too, but Angel explained to her that she couldn't up and leave, because it was customary to sit and allow people to offer their condolences. *These people are phony. They just want to look me in the eye and rejoice in my pain.*

Angel lovingly gave her a pair of dark sunglasses—her Angel thought of everything—and patted her hand as the mourners passed by, expressing their sorrow. Alma simply nodded. She didn't even look at most of them.

She stared at Harold in the casket, wishing he would sit up and tell her he was only kidding. She grieved over every bad word she'd ever said to him and wished she could take them all back. Death was real. We agreed marriage was *till death do you part*, but we never put a face on death, so it didn't sound quite so bad.

Alma now saw the face of death, and it scared the hell out of her. What had she gotten herself into? Death was supposed to come in threes, an old wives' tale. It never comes for only one person. Threes. She wanted to be the second of the three right now and wished she could be taken, because it hurt too much to be alive. Todd squeezed her hand to signal that someone was talking to her.

"Momma, it's Ms. Cartwright."

"I'm so sorry about your loss. Harold was a good man. If there's anything I can do, please let me know. I'll be happy to do it," Ms. Cartwright said.

You can get out of my face, Alma thought, then nodded and looked to Todd, sitting to her right. She couldn't for the life of her figure out why he had brought that white woman of his to a black church up in Harlem, but she was glad he'd come home nonetheless. Alma smiled at him, thinking he looked just like his daddy. A new, improved version of Harold. Todd had all his teeth, unlike Jesse, who was missing an upper front tooth. He looked like his father's side of the family, but everyone said he was the spitting image of her, in many ways and for many reasons.

Todd could have done much better than the *thing* sitting next to him, she thought. Hadn't she taught him about the civil rights marches she used to participate in? Todd's children, the mutts, had gotten a lot bigger than they were in the pictures he sent.

Alma rolled her eyes as Angel's husband, Darryl, a.k.a. Fatso, waddled past her. She was glad for the shades, because her eyes couldn't hide her contempt for him. They'd had a little spat earlier in the day, because he kept digging his huge hands in the pots of food Angel was preparing. When his finger dipped into the barbecued ribs, well, that did it.

"How big do you want to get?" she'd demanded.

"I'm hungry," he'd said between chewing, swallowing, and reaching for more.

"You stay hungry. I've never seen somebody do aerobics running from pot to pot like you. Listen to you chomping on them bones like a wild boar. You making me lose my appetite."

"Talk to your mother, Angel," he'd warned.

"What are you going to do? I'll throw the chicken in the middle of the street and watch you get hit by a car trying to pick it up."

"Momma, please be nice," Angel had begged.

"OK. I'll be nice. Darryl, please get your fat ass out of my kitchen so we can save some food for the guests, the invited ones."

He had taken offense but grabbed some more pieces of ribs and left the kitchen, telling Angel they should go.

"Angel was invited!" Alma had yelled after him.

He hated her, and she hated him, but the rules of a funeral say that you have to put your feelings aside and pay honor to the survivors of the deceased.

* * *

"Momma, can I talk to you?" Jesse asked at the reception.

"Sure, baby."

"Not here. Can we go in the bedroom?" Alma nodded. She would have to face the bedroom eventually.

In her mind's eye, she relived Harold's cold, stiff body lying on the now empty bedframe. Todd and Angel had dragged the mattress outside, because Alma was too spooked to enter the room with it still there.

"What is it, Jesse?"

"Momma, I know this may be bad timing, but Daddy said he was going to give me money so I can get that trumpet. Did he leave me anything?"

"Yes, son. A swift kick in the ass, and I'm going to give it to you right now if you dare fix your junkie mouth to ask me something that insensitive again," Alma replied.

She knew it had to be more than reefers he was smoking to be that disrespectful. That's why she hated these funereal rituals, because of stupid people like him not knowing how to act. Jesse was lucky Rae Ann picked that moment to walk through the front door sporting a red miniskirt. Alma turned her attention to the noise in the living room. When she saw the perpetrator of the commotion, it took all of Alma's children to restrain her as she snatched up her butcher knife.

"Don't change your clothes, folks, because there's going to be two funerals tonight," she said determinedly.

"Why are you doing this, Alma? What did I ever do

to you?" Rae Ann's voice was slurred. She was drunk and probably wanted some closure. "I only want to pay my respects," Rae Ann drawled.

Alma hated her. Todd begged Rae Ann to leave, but she demanded a quick drink first. Alma threw a bottle of vodka at her head, and she ducked as the bottle splashed its contents all over her exposed legs. That was all the drink she was going to get.

"You're going to be drinking your own blood after I cut your throat, you little two-bit tramp. Get your bleached-blond ass out of here."

"Fine! I'll leave. What goes around come back around, Alma," Rae Ann warned as she defiantly turned and left.

Harold's brother, Fred, watched this drama unfold.

"She gave Harold that heart attack," he whispered to several non-family members, loudly enough for Alma to overhear. "I live three blocks from here," he went on. "I know how much stress she put poor Harold through. He would come by all hours of the night, complaining how Alma locked him out or called the cops to make him get out his own home. Leave her. That's all I'd tell him. Now look what's happened."

This particular clique of guests murmured their agreement. Alma was livid. Angel squeezed her hand.

" 'I can't leave,' Harold would say. 'She needs me,'" Fred said mockingly. "I asked him what he was doing on my couch, then, if she needs him so badly. 'She just needs a little space till the morning,' he'd say. Can you believe this?

Next thing you know, the sun's up, and Alma's waiting outside my place with a hot cup of coffee and buttered roll for him. It was the strangest relationship I've ever seen, but thank God I won't have to bear witness no more. This is the last time I'll ever have to look her in those squinty eyes. Good-bye and good riddance."

I've still got my butcher knife, little Freddy. Better watch your tongue, she thought.

When the guests had departed, Angel helped her mother pull out the couch and make her bed.

"Lay next to me until I fall asleep," Alma said through the moans and groans of her aching body trying to dodge the springs poking through the pancake-thin mattress. The reality of sleeping alone made her cry again. "I want him back."

"So do I, Momma."

"How could God do this to me?" she asked her Angel.

"Sometimes God allows us to be tested, Momma, but he will never put anything before us that we can't handle. You have to be strong."

"It's going to be hard, baby. I've been with him for forty-four years. I don't know who I am without him."

"I know," Angel said as she stroked Alma's freshly dyed hair. "I want you to come live with us for a while."

"I can't do that, Angel."

"Why not?"

"There's not enough room for you, me, and Fatso in that house. Actually, there isn't enough room for him and nobody in that house." They both laughed.

"You're crazy, Momma."

"I'm going to stay right here. I'll be fine. It will take some time, but your momma is strong. My daddy didn't raise no punks," Alma joked. "I'll be fine. This, too, shall pass, so the good Lord says."

chapter five

A week had passed since the funeral, and life was hard for Alma with no friends and no routine. She spent most of her time gazing out the window, buzzed by the stronger dosage of Valium prescribed for her anxiety attacks. Still, panic invaded and consumed the tiniest of tasks Alma set out to accomplish.

Something as simple as folding laundry would lead her mind to wondering what she would do for extra money now that Harold's pension was cut off. How could she keep a roof over her head and not be a burden to her children? Would this feeling of overwhelming guilt ever pass, or would it haunt her for the rest of her existence?

These were the questions playing on a loop in her mind.

The only temporary fix was the dulling effects of the drugs. They helped to shut off her receptor.

To make matters worse, Alma had anxiety about becoming an addict like Jesse, whom she had recently threatened to slap with a restraining order. He had come by the house seemingly to look after her.

"Momma, I wanna be here for you. It's not good for you to be alone right now," he had said convincingly. "Let me stay here, do the chores around the house, run errands, and cook for you."

"Thank you, son."

No sooner had he moved in than Alma noticed things were moving out. One day, she had dashed into her bedroom after a long walk, recommended by Jesse, to find one of Harold's cufflinks on the floor. It was from his twenty-four-karat-gold square set, the one with his initials, H.S.W. She had picked it up to put it back in the dresser drawer and saw that all of Harold's jewelry was gone. Alma knew right away that Jesse was the culprit. He had even taken Harold's wedding ring. Probably pawned it for God knew how little money.

When he came back that night wearing a new pair of jeans, he had lied and said he didn't know what happened to the jewelry. The next day, Jesse had been busted trying to cash one of Harold's pension checks. Alma had wanted to press charges, but how could a mother put her son in jail? *What would people think?*

"I'm ashamed to call myself your mother. You are no

longer welcome in my house, and if you do come around, I will take my knife and cut you to the fat meat," Alma had warned.

"I'm sorry. I just wanted to get that horn," he'd said through crocodile tears.

"You're sorry, all right. Now, get on out of here!"

On the other hand, Angel called her on a regular basis to make certain she was doing all right.

"Hey, Momma, do you need anything? Are you taking your medicine? Are you sure you don't want to come to Texas for a spell?"

"No, baby, Momma is fine," she always said. She wasn't, but she didn't want her daughter to worry, so she lied. Angel had enough to occupy her time. Between the new baby and the baby elephant she called a husband, her plate was full.

Todd was a real disappointment. He had left the day after the funeral.

"I had to go," Todd's tinny voice had echoed from his cell phone in Germany.

"You just barely said hello, son, and then the quickest of good-byes."

"I didn't have the time. This trip wasn't exactly planned. Everything was so sudden. We were running late for the plane. It's hard traveling with kids. We couldn't wake them because they were jet-lagged from the trip over. Plus, my job expected me back for an important project I'm heading up."

Todd had presented every legitimate excuse in the

book, but Alma blamed the white girl. She had his head all messed up. He was under her control. Alma believed the *wet dog* was against her because she had asked her not to leave her stringy blond hair all over the bathroom sink. Alma was also pissed that Wet Dog had used her good hairbrush and ended up giving it to Helga as a gift. Their leaving like that was her way of showing Alma who the real boss was, snatching her son off to another world when he needed to be with his mother.

Alma noticed that Rae Ann kept her drapes closed since Harold had died. *No one else wants to see those ten-inch titties.*

The radio was her only friend. It amazed her how vivid the brain was, how a song could pull up not only images but smells and emotions, too.

She caught herself many times having one-sided conversations with Harold. It was funny how long she would be talking, not even expecting a reaction, because that was the relationship they had. She talked, he didn't.

Alma decided the best thing to do was to put all of his belongings into boxes and either store them or give it all to charity. It was easy to find his things, since Alma relegated all of his worldly possessions to three areas: a dresser drawer in the bedroom, one small section of her closet, and the front hallway closet, where he kept his suits, hats, and jackets. Harold had never complained about the arrangement.

"If it makes you happy, it makes me happy. I don't need

anything else to wear. I'll just clothe myself in your love," he had told her after she expressed how bad she felt that he didn't have more space.

Alma put his favorite burgundy fedora on her head, smoothing out the brim and pulling it down to cover her right eye the way Harold used to wear it. This was the hat he had worn the first and only time they went to the opera. It was the middle of winter, and a customer at Harold's second job as night watchman at a construction site had given him two tickets to *Madame Butterfly*. They hadn't been on a date in a while thanks to the call of parenthood, so they'd jumped at the chance to get out of the house. It was freezing cold as they walked from the train station toward the Majestic Theatre on Broadway.

"We're never going to make it in time if you don't walk a little faster, Alma."

"These shoes are hurting my feet, Harold. Why don't you carry me?" she'd joked.

Harold hated being late. Alma didn't mind making an entrance.

"We're already ten minutes late. Mr. Raven said we had to be on time for this thing," Harold had reminded her.

When they'd finally arrived at the Majestic, the doors were closed, and the usher told them they would have to wait until the intermission to be seated. That would be in an hour.

"One hour!" Alma had exclaimed. "What are we supposed to do for an hour?"

"You are welcome to go to the bar area," the usher had offered.

They'd gone to a bar but not the one at the theater. Alma had needed to sit.

Now, she placed a couple of pairs of Harold's shoes in a box and noticed for the first time that the heels on both right shoes were worn down more than the left ones. In fact, all of his shoes were worn like that. It must have been from the scoliosis, which tilted his spine slightly to the right as he grew older. Harold had been able to mask the defect by shifting it into a cool gait in his walk.

His shirts, sweaters, ties, and socks—even his underwear—all had the same smell. They smelled like him. The scent God made just for him that only a wife, a lover, or a friend would know. Being all three intensified the experience for Alma. She held his worn undershirt to her face and inhaled deeply. She cried softly and let the fabric absorb her tears.

Alma opened the hall closet to find Harold's jacket on the floor. She remembered him standing in the stairwell, looking back at her with the jacket in hand. The memory was vivid—he had switched the jacket into the other hand to grab hold of the banister that guided him safely from her gaze.

As Alma folded the lightweight, faded blue blazer, she felt something tucked away in the breast pocket. She searched and found the tickets to the dance Harold was going to take her to for her birthday. She had forgotten she was turning the big six-five tomorrow. She had bought herself a beautiful red satin dress she found in a going-out-of-business sale, in case Harold had wanted to take her out. He was always surprising her on birthdays. "Just be ready," he would say.

He'd never tell her what he was planning, because she would be disappointed, never happy once she knew. He had decided early on that he would always surprise her. Alma liked surprises—they were romantic to her—and loved to dance. After all the years of anger and resentment, they still had terrific chemistry on the dance floor. He was in control of her movements, and she submitted to his direction, but only under the flashing colored lights.

Alma thought about going to the dance by herself but quickly dismissed that idea, imagining people staring at her, asking, "Who's the old lady standing in the puddle of tears?" Alma wished she could pop another Valium to calm the anxiety that was creeping into her heart.

"My daddy didn't raise no punks!" she reassured herself. She had promised herself not to take any more of the pills, because they only increased the anxiety when they wore off. From now on, she was going to deal with whatever life threw her way.

Alma slept for twelve hours, and when she woke, she felt exhausted, depressed, and unable to go back to sleep. She realized that was how doctors got you addicted. They made you believe the only thing to stop the hurt was to take another pill.

No, she told herself as she put the phone down after dialing the doctor's office to request a refill. She was determined to give them up and decided to drink some coffee and take a long walk to help clear her head.

Alma was sipping her second cup of Folgers when the doorbell rang. Standing outside was a deliveryman with a beautiful bouquet of pink roses and bird-of-paradise, a rich variation of a rainbow. They were from Harold! The stranger had to hold her up when she collapsed in his arms, crying like a baby.

How did he send flowers from the grave? Harold must have known his time was short and was taking delight in tormenting her. Wasn't his death enough? Why couldn't he have had a little heart attack to teach her this lesson? She would have taken care of him and helped nurse him back to health with her special chicken noodle soup. Harold hated hospital food. If he'd had a small attack, she could have recognized her sins and changed her contrary ways. Instead, he left her with nothing but all this damn guilt! The flowers only poured salt on the wound.

Alma decided she could no longer bear this tortured state.

Dearest Children,

It's with love and tears that I write this letter to say my good-byes. I can't take the pain any longer.

It's too hard. It's just too damn hard for me to move on. I always believed I was tough and would get through this, but now I know I can't. I can't because I know what your father knows, which is that I killed him. I killed your father with unkind words, unspoken rage, and a jealous heart that all the love in the world couldn't tame. I only pray God judges me kinder than I've judged myself. Now it's time to give life for life. Be it heaven or hell, I must join your father wherever death takes me and beg for his forgiveness. It's the only way to quiet the accuser yelling "Murderer!" in my mind. This is not a suicide note. Rather, it is a farewell to misery, bon voyage to pain, adios to grief statement. Don't feel bad for me. I will be at peace. Yes, peace. That's what I want right now.

Todd, honey, I'm going to hold my tongue about your little "wet dog" and only hope she's not standing next to you reading my business—serves her right if she is. Todd, thank you for turning out to be such a fine young man. You make your mother proud in every way. My Angel, baby, I don't want to be any more of a weight around your neck than the ton of a husband you already got. Know Momma loves you more than this life. Jesse, you've got to give your life over to Christ and step up to be the great man I know you can still be. I've left you a tiny bit of money to help with lessons so you can stop sounding like a raggedy bugle boy. I'll miss you all.

Love,
Momma

P.S. Make sure they put a smile on my face and bury me next to your daddy, so that if he looks over, he'll see that he's the only one who makes me happy.

Alma sealed the envelope with the rest of her tears.

She turned the radio up. She took a long hot bath, made up her face, and put on the red satin dress she bought for her birthday, determined to look and smell good when they found her. Alma pulled the petals from the pink roses and laid them out on a gold silk sheet she draped over the couch. She poured herself a glass of red wine after turning the gas oven on. She gulped the first, then poured a second full glass to sip on as she faded away. Alma took her favorite seat at the living-room window, humming along to the song that was playing on the radio. How ironic. It was Marvin Gaye's "If I Should Die Tonight"! Alma laughed because she couldn't cry anymore.

Thank God it would soon be over. She saw the group of six or seven women in red hats passing along the opposite side of the street. One of them, a white woman, looked up and waved at her.

Feeling the effects of the wine-and-gas concoction,

Alma waved back. Her head was very light, and she decided it was time to go lie down on the couch. She stood up and immediately fell forward, hitting her head on the windowsill.

Good-bye, you cold, cruel world, Alma thought as she felt warm blood oozing from the top of her head.

chapter six

Delilah Samson hated hospitals as much as she hated her name. It was an inside joke that her devout Christian parents thought was clever and cute. It was supposed to remind Delilah of her spiritual roots. What it really did was become a thorn in their daughter's side for her entire childhood. The boys were afraid of her name's biblical history and teased poor Delilah about being a betrayer of man. The girls in her suburban neighborhood labeled her a threat to their prepubescent boyfriends and literally ran from her whenever she came around. The only friends she had were the black family that lived on the edge of town that separated the "good" neighborhood from the "bad" one.

Being a diabetic, it made her sick to see the nurse inject the IV needle into Alma's arm. Needles were her life. Five times a day, she had to prick her finger to check her sugar levels. Then, before every meal, she had to inject herself in the stomach with 2.2 units of insulin. The worst part of the disease was having to give herself the needle. The doctor told her she would get used to it. That was seven years ago. Delilah was still waiting for acceptance.

Alma opened her eyes, expecting to see Jesus in such a bright white room. Instead, she saw an angel. Her daughter, Angel, was standing over her with a serious expression on her face.

"Are you all right, Momma?"

"My head hurts," Alma replied weakly.

"You had to get some stitches, and there's a very nasty bump under that wrap. The doctor said you will be fine in a few days."

"How did I get here? How long has it been?"

"You've been here all day. These nice women over here found you." She pointed to the women wearing red hats, sitting patiently in a corner of the hospital room.

Alma noticed a little bit of everything had gone into the making of the hats—silk ribbon, tulle, beading, and yard after yard of material. One of them stood up. She was white and had a big, round, pretty face with an unhealthy yellowish color to her skin, like uncooked chicken.

"My name is Delilah, but my friends call me Sister Dee, and these are Sisters Joy, Stephanie, Sarah, Yvette, and Magdalena." The ladies smiled and waved hello at the calling of their names. "We are the Red Hatters."

"We were walking by and saw you fall against the window. We had to break down the door to get to you. Some fool left the gas on! But don't you worry your dear heart, Sisters May and Aubrey are there now, making sure the place gets aired out and the door gets fixed. They will leave your key with the building manager."

"Did you go through my stuff?" Alma asked accusingly.

"Why, of course not," Sister Dee replied.

"Momma, be nice," Angel whispered through clenched teeth.

Alma rolled her eyes, dismissing the chastisement. "How'd you get here so fast if no one went looking through my stuff?"

"I called the house to wish you a happy birthday, and one of the Red Hats, Sister Joy, I believe, told me there was an accident and police were in your house, so I hopped the first plane I could to come see you. Now, why don't you thank these nice ladies for being kind enough to look out for you, Momma?"

"Thank you," Alma said.

"You are quite welcome. Anyway, we just wanted to make sure you were OK. We'll be getting on now and will certainly keep you in our prayers. Take care," Dee said, and she beckoned the others to leave.

Alma and Angel sat in silence as the women left.

"I want to go home," Alma said, attempting to sit up. The pain in her head prevented any real movement.

"You're not going anywhere right now! And when you do leave here, you are coming home with me."

"I don't want to go to Texas."

"I'm not asking you, I'm telling you! Suicide, Momma? No, I already made the arrangements."

"You know I don't fly."

Angel showed her two Greyhound bus tickets.

"What about Chubbsy Wubbsy? What's he going to say about this?" Alma asked.

"Darryl said it would be fine with him."

"He really said that?"

"Yes. He understands our bond, and besides, if he didn't like it, he'd have to lump it elsewhere," Angel said defiantly. Alma liked this strong will of hers. It reminded her of her own self.

"I'm not giving up my apartment! All my children were born and raised there."

"I'm not saying you have to give up nothing. I just think you need to get away from all the memories for a while, until you have a chance to heal. Some sunshine and fresh country air will do you good."

"How long is a while?" Alma asked.

"Three months."

"I was thinking three weeks. You know me and Fatso won't make it past three days."

"You certainly won't if you keep calling him Fatso, Momma."

"I'll work on it. How's my favorite grandbaby?"

"Nia is great and so happy her grandma is coming to live with her."

"Well, if you had said that to begin with, we wouldn't need to be having this conversation," Alma joked.

It took four days to get to Texas, because Alma kept complaining about the smell and the speed and the route of the bus. They got off twice to check into a hotel so Alma could bathe and get a little sleep. Angel had the patience of Job, and flying was not an option. When they arrived in Texas, Fatso met them at the station. He was obviously not happy about Alma's visit.

"Hello, Darryl," Alma said exactly the way she had rehearsed it with Angel. "Where's my grandbaby?"

"I left her in the car," Darryl said.

"You left her in the car? You must be stupider than you look, man," Alma fired back. "You're not supposed to leave a child unattended in a car!"

"The car is right there," he said, pointing to a white SUV parked a few feet from them.

"Momma, apologize."

Alma didn't. She simply dropped her bags at his feet and hurried to the car to see Nia strapped safely in the car seat. Darryl shook his head and gave his wife a nasty look as he picked up the bags and threw them into the back of the SUV. Angel stopped him before he climbed into the driver's seat and gave him a loving hug. Alma pretended not to notice this public display of affection. Darryl caught her sneaking a peek and used it as an opportunity to slap her back by gently kissing the top of his wife's head.

Alma did not like sleeping in the den. It hurt her back to sleep on that rock-hard mattress in the pull-out couch. And the sheets felt sandy. Plus, the noise from the fan spinning over her head kept her awake.

Darryl helped Angel rearrange the baby's room to accommodate her, but Alma complained that the bed was too small, and it made her feel as if she was suffocating in that tiny room. The only other choice was the master bedroom, which Darryl said "Hell no" to. Angel reminded him that this was her mother and they should make the small sacrifice in her time of mourning. Darryl reluctantly gave in, but it cost Angel plenty of arguments in the middle of the night. Alma would sleep through most of them in their luxurious custom bed. She had never seen such a large bed before. It was a double king, which Darryl took up half of.

In the mornings, Alma tried to help out around the house by cooking breakfast for everyone. Angel appreciated it, but Darryl resented the strict diet Alma had put him on. She would make him only two pancakes, as opposed to the six he normally had. She said if he moved more and ate less, he might be able to do more than lie on top of his wife at night. In keeping with the spirit of moving more, Alma would leave his clothing on the floor for him to bend over and pick up, to help burn a few calories.

Darryl started to stay out late to avoid seeing Alma. He said she was mean as hell and pure evil, even in her sleep, which was the only way he would be in the house with her.

One night, he came home drunk and got into it with Angel. When Alma tried to get involved, Angel told her to back off and let them work out their own problems. Alma didn't listen, so Darryl grabbed her by the robe and threatened to punch all her teeth out. Angel pulled his own gun on him and told him she would kill him if he didn't let her mother go. Darryl came to his senses, broke down into tears, and walked out of the house.

"Maybe you should go to a nursing home, Momma. At least you can make some friends there." Angel made her mother a cup of Folgers to help steady her nerves.

"I'm a young woman. I'm not going to live in no damn nursing home," Alma replied.

"Then why don't you go live with Todd? He said you could stay in his guesthouse. It's a beautiful one-bedroom and has a full kitchen, with a garden outside where you can grow your own vegetables."

"First of all, I'm not getting on an airplane and going nowhere. Them death cylinders crash all the time! And it's not like you can stand on the side of the road and call another when it breaks down. Look, Angel, I appreciate you opening up your home to me, but I know when my welcome's done. I'll head back home. It's time."

"You can't go home, Momma. Let me talk to Darryl, okay? We'll work something out," Angel reassured her.

Alma knew her time was up. In the middle of the night, she packed her bags, called a cab, and went to the bus station. Alma could see Angel watching from her darkened bedroom window, crying. It was best to leave.

On the bus ride home, Alma thought about some of the things Angel had said to her.

"Momma, life is a short ride, and the journey is easier to enjoy if you don't carry so much luggage. Give those bags of burden to God, and try to open up and let people into your circle so you can start enjoying life. Don't die a bitter woman. Be a better woman."

Angel had a way of speaking to Alma's heart. She didn't pull punches. Alma knew beyond a doubt that she loved her Angel, who only wanted what was best for her.

But how do you open up when you can't trust anyone? When you feel the whole world is against you? When every time you try to let your guard down, you get a slap in the face? Alma knew Angel was right, but having friends wasn't in the cards for her.

Angel begged her to try to work on softening her heart by reading the leather-bound Bible she gave her for her birthday, reminding her that the world was against Jesus, too, and he allowed love to conquer the world. Alma would only respond by saying that Jesus was a whole mess better than her.

"If they had spit on me back then and I had all the powers he had, I would have turned them into bloated green frogs and then squished them under my sandals. Nobody is going to slap me and get away with it. If I have to turn the other cheek, it will be to show them which side of my ass to kiss."

Alma did like the story of Jonah. She believed it proved God had a sense of humor. He told Jonah to deliver a message of judgment to the people of Nineveh, but Jonah was frightened of what people would think of him. He ran away and caught a boat in the opposite direction of the city. God caused a huge storm to fall upon the boat, and the people threw Jonah overboard because he claimed God was after him. Sure enough, a massive, slimy fish swallowed him up. After three days of Jonah's prayers in the fish's belly, God had the fish spit him out near the city of Nineveh, which he was to condemn. The moral of the story, Alma thought, was that you were going to do what God said to do whether you liked it or not!

Alma noticed the colorful leaves that decorated the tops of trees and the sides of the road. Fall was one of her favorite times of the year, because it reminded her of school when she was young, innocent, and full of hope. Being a good student came easily for Alma, having had a mother who taught English. Alma loved creative writing. She had received a full liberal arts scholarship from Brandeis University after winning several awards for her poetry and short stories. She remembered her favorite piece, called "The Girl Who Could Fly." It was about this little girl who discovered she had the power to fly, and when people found out, they wanted to operate on her to understand how she did it. They paid her parents to give her up to science. The little girl flew away to a small town far away from everyone she knew and loved. Vowing never to fly again, she lived as an unhappy mortal until she met a boy who could fly, too. Together they traveled the world and lived happily ever after. Alma wondered why and how she had given up something she loved doing so dearly. How did she go from spending her day having tea parties with her favorite doll, Macy—because that's where she was bought, Macy's—making up fantastic stories about things she never knew and places she'd never been, to being this angry old woman who barely could get through the day no matter how beautiful it was? She missed that little girl in her.

What happened to her, Alma? Did you kill her, too? she wondered, promising God that she would make it her mission to reclaim her joy.

When Alma arrived at her apartment, she found a package in front of her door. It was from the Red Hats. Inside was a beautiful antique black doll dressed in a purple dress, with a blood-red hat on her head. Alma loved to collect dolls. Her house was full of them. The obsession stemmed from a childhood where she grew up extremely poor and had only one doll to play with. She lost Macy on a school trip, and her father wouldn't buy another because he said she shouldn't have brought it to school. Alma promised herself that when she grew up, she was going to buy herself every doll she had ever seen. Well, almost every one. She hated her father. The man never had a kind word to say, and she couldn't remember him ever hugging her or telling Alma he loved her. A card came with the package.

Dear Alma,

It was a pleasure meeting you and Angel. All the sisters enjoyed spending a little time with Angel. You certainly named her right. She is an intelligent, sweet, and kind young woman who loves her mother. We know the apple doesn't fall far from the tree. We noticed you collect antique dolls and thought you would like this one. May God continue to bless you and yours.

In love,
Sister Dee and the Red Hats!

Alma liked the card, because it had a beautiful red hat embroidered on the front of it. She liked how silky it felt, very classy. There was also an invitation to a book fair in the park that weekend.

Alma tossed the invitation onto the kitchen table, thinking it and the doll were just a scam to get her to come and spend her hard-earned money at their book fair. She hated anyone who tried to hustle her. Did they think she was born yesterday? She told herself she would be damned if she'd go to that book fair.

Alma sat at the kitchen table, sipping a hot cup of chamomile tea Angel had turned her on to in Texas. It relaxed her and didn't make her feel groggy the way the pills did. Although she was drinking the tea, she felt cold. She noticed a breeze billow the curtains above the sink. As she went to close the window, Alma slipped on the multicolored rag rug and slammed back-first to the floor. She lay there unable to get up, moaning and asking God to help her. The moans turned to tears, and she asked God to take her.

"What did I do to you, God? Why are you doing this to me? Why couldn't you just let me die? What do you want from me?" she screamed to heaven.

A strong breeze whisked into the kitchen, blowing the book-fair flyer off the table and onto the floor next to her.

chapter seven

Alma limped through Morningside Park toward the group of Red Hats stationed at the book fair. Her body ached from the fall. She hadn't felt this kind of full-body soreness since getting hit by a car at fourteen.

Alma remembered that day clearly, because she was dressed up and skipping her way to Sunday school. Her mother had warned her about running in her good church clothes, so, wanting to be obedient, she'd split the difference between running and walking by skipping real fast. Alma felt she could justify it without technically being a liar. That was mistake number one. The bigger mistake was not going the normal route to church. She had found a nickel and wanted to stop and get some penny candies to help pass the time at the two-hour sit-down. Back then, a nickel bought a lot of treats. Alma had a difficult time picking which candy she wanted—the shoestring licorice, Kool-Aid stick or the taffy and chocolate cherries—settling on one of each. She'd realized she was running late for service, and that would cost her a spanking, so after sucking down the Kool-Aid stick to give her the energy to skip the six blocks, she took a shortcut past the liquor store that had a German shepherd that was notorious for chasing anyone who ran past the store. The owner used to keep the door open to save on his air-conditioning bill. The mean old dog was kept on a long leash that stopped just short of the door. As Alma skipped past the store, the dog had given chase, barking loudly and almost giving her a heart attack. Alma had forgotten the dog was on its chain and couldn't get out of the store. She had run into the street to avoid the long fangs coming her way. As soon as she stepped off the curb, a taxi had slammed into her, separating Alma from her candy.

"So glad you could make it, Alma." Sister Dee greeted her now. "What happened to your leg?"

"Oh, it's nothing. I lost my balance trying to open a window. I'll be all right."

"Alma, none of us are getting any younger. I fell down last month. I was just standing up, and the next thing I know, I'm on the ground. The doctor said it was my blood sugar. He said my diabetes is getting worse, so now he's put me on these medications that make me so tired I need sugar just to stay awake. Come on, let me show you around, introduce you to some more of the girls."

Alma was impressed by the different ethnicities of the Red Hats. She'd been sure this was a group of women from some black church who hung out together. She was wrong. Sister Dee explained that the founder of the club, Sue Ellen Cooper, was a white woman who wanted to bring a bunch of women over the age of fifty together to have fun and prove that life begins after your maternal duties end.

The book fair was a way for the women to raise money to travel and help out the less fortunate Red Hats.

"We're going to Atlantic City next month, and we need some money for chips to gamble, right, girls?" Dee said.

"Yes, Queen Mother!" Joy shouted back.

Alma did not like hearing this black woman addressing a white woman as her queen and mother! It turned her stomach, reminding her of the white woman she used to work for. Mrs. Albertson was an old, angry, racist witch who had lorded her power over Alma as if she were her slave. She'd insisted on being called Madame Albertson. If Alma was a minute late, she would deduct an hour's pay, even though she knew Alma had a young child at home and was pregnant with another. Mrs. Albertson hadn't cared if Alma was tired, sick, or even dead—she was determined to get a full day's work out of her. That included thoroughly cleaning the refrigerator every day, hand-washing the toilet, and waxing the floor on her hands and knees weekly. If the house was clean, she would toss all her clothing on the floor and have Alma redo the closet. Sometimes she would request it to be color-coordinated, and then after two weeks or so, she would complain that she couldn't find a particular dress and accuse Alma of stealing it. She would deduct that from her pay, too, threatening to fire her if she didn't reimburse her. Alma had needed the job too much to quit, but working for that woman was hell. It got to a point where Alma would break down and cry, begging that woman to forgive her for taking the dress she knew she didn't have, just to keep the job. Mrs. Albertson had seemed to get some sort of sick enjoyment out of breaking Alma down. She would stare at her with her cold blue eyes and a little smirk on her face as she "considered" whether to accept the tearful apology or not. Sometimes the Grinch would wait until Alma finished mopping the floor, then walk over it wet and have her do it again because she saw footprints. What made this old crow so evil Alma could never figure out, but fear of being out of a job reminded Alma to hold her tongue. She would repeat those words in her head throughout the day—*Hold your tongue*—and a voice in her head would shout back, *Holding our tongues kept us in slavery for two hundred years!* One of the happiest days of her life was the one when she quit working for old Madame Albertson. Alma had waited until her boss lady went out for her daily walk, then washed all of her dark clothes in bleach, mopped the floor in molasses, and for good measure, stopped up the toilet with a brown paper bag, took a dump, and left it without flushing. Madame Albertson had come home to find Alma sitting on her couch and watching television.

"What the hell do you think you are doing?" Mrs. Albertson had demanded.

Alma had walked right up to the elderly demon. "I'm liberating myself from your slavery, you old bitch. I wanted to thank you for nothing and let you know I left you a little gift in the bathroom. I made it myself, and it looks just like you."

Alma had whistled as she waltzed out that door for the last time.

"Why do you call her Queen Mother?" Alma now asked Joy sharply.

"Oh, we all give each other nicknames in the Red Hats," Joy replied.

What's yours, Sister Slave-a-lot? Alma wondered to herself.

"Delilah is Queen Mother because she started this chapter of the Red Hats."

"You mean there's more?"

"Oh, yes, we are a global sisterhood. If you travel anywhere in the world, you can find a chapter of Red Hats that will welcome you with big smiles and open arms," Queen Mother said.

"Really? Is it part of the mandate to sell books?" Alma inquired.

Magdalena picked up on where Alma was going with her line of questioning. "Honey, we don't work for no one.

We formed a book club where we read one book a month and then meet for tea to discuss whatever it was we read."

"We had some really heated debates recently regarding a book titled *The Fire Next Time* by James Baldwin," Dee said proudly.

Alma knew this book well. It was one of her favorites. Baldwin had predicted an intervention by God in the near future for the mistreatment of black folks in America. What Alma wanted to know was what Dee knew about black folks and their pain.

"I bet I know what side of the debate you were on," Alma said.

"I'll bet you you're wrong. Hell, Sister Dee is just as black as one of us." Joy laughed.

"Yeah, until the cops come. Then I bet she gets real white," Alma shot back.

Sister Dee laughed off the insult. "I think it's healthy to keep our minds active while searching for creative solutions to the world's problems. Most of us have children and grandchildren who have no clue what was suffered for them to have the opportunities they now take for granted. But mostly, this is just *Sex and the City* for old biddies," Dee joked.

Alma enjoyed her day in the park with the Red Hats and ended up purchasing several books, although she promised herself she would not be conned. As she approached her building, she noticed there were police cars in front of it.

"I live in this building. What's going on here?" she asked the young black officer.

"There's been a mugging, ma'am," he said.

"Who?"

"It was the building manager, ma'am."

"Mrs. Johnson?"

"Yes. Two men broke in, beat her, tied her up, and robbed her. I suggest you lock your door and make sure you know who it is before you open up for any visitors," he said.

"Did you catch them?"

"Not yet, ma'am. Please be careful. If you notice anything suspicious, please give me a call. My name is Officer Davis. My number is on this card," he said, handing Alma his card.

She wished he would stop calling her ma'am. It made her feel ancient.

"She's going to be all right, isn't she?" Alma asked.

"We certainly hope so, ma'am."

Alma shook her head in disbelief as she made her way through the crowd and up the stairs. She could only think about how unsafe she felt in this building with all the steps to climb if someone was after her. Alma told herself she might make it up the first flight on adrenaline, but she knew she was too out of shape to get up four long flights with someone chasing her. Alma put her books in the apartment and went to check on poor Mrs. Johnson.

Why would someone do such a bad thing to such a good woman? Mrs. Johnson was the sweetest person Alma knew. Never had a cross word to say about anyone and cared about everyone. If she saw a homeless person begging, she would pay them to sweep the front of the building. If she witnessed any of the neighborhood kids getting into trouble, she would be the first to give them an earful about being a better person.

Alma made Mrs. Johnson a pot of her famous chicken noodle soup and a cup of chamomile tea with lemon and honey.

"Thank you so much, Alma."

"It is my pleasure, Mrs. Johnson. You get some rest now, and if you need anything, don't be shy about giving me a call," she said before leaving.

Alma locked the door and slid the chain in the slot. All of a sudden, she missed Harold even more. Regardless of how they might have outwardly treated each other, Alma was never afraid with him around, because she knew he would fight to the death for her. A good night's sleep was out of the question now. Alma was armed with a cast-iron frying pan that she placed on the night table by her medicine. By her side was a hammer, under her pillow her trusty butcher knife. It was not going to be easy to tie her up and rob her. She practiced grabbing the strategically placed weapons.

* * *

Morning couldn't come fast enough. Alma was dressed and ready to get out as soon as she saw sunlight. She walked to the grocery store to get a cup of coffee and a buttered roll. She enjoyed them on a bench outside the park. She fought the voice in her head that said, *Leave now, and forget those catty red-hatted women. It's only going to end up hurting again.* Women were generally not to be trusted in Alma's world.

But the only alternative was to go back home, where she was a prisoner of her own fears. After reading the Red Hats' weekly schedule, Alma decided she would conveniently be at the Marie Callender's before the ladies arrived for lunch. If they asked her to join them, she would. When she arrived, Alma quickly realized that these were women with nothing to do but eat, and they were already there. For a moment, Alma thought to run away, but Sister Dee spotted her as she strolled past the restaurant a second time. They waved her inside and made space for her to sit next to Dee.

"You look so beautiful, Alma. Don't she look good?" Magdalena asked the group.

"Yes, she does," Dee said.

All of the women except Joy complimented Alma on her outfit and her hair, which she soaked up. She needed reassurance, especially having been up all night.

"Why, thank you, ladies."

Dee was eating a big slice of hot apple pie à la mode. "Would you like some of this pie, baby? We have apple, pumpkin, sweet potato, or pecan."

"No, thank you. I'll just have some tea. I thought you were diabetic. Are you supposed to be eating pie?" Alma asked.

"If you ask the doctor, I'm not supposed to do nothing fun anymore. I've got to have my pie. I'll just drink a little green tea later to balance out my sugar," Dee confided.

"That works?"

"Only in her mind," Joy joked.

"Oh, hush up and let me do me," Dee snapped back.

"They already threatened to cut your foot off. I'm just looking out for you. You're the one that's going to be hopping around, not me," Joy said as she bit into a piping-hot piece of pecan pie.

"Anyway, Alma, how are you doing today?" Dee queried.

"I don't know. Good, I guess."

"You guess? Either you is or you ain't," Magdalena said.

Alma was too tired to put Magdalena in her place. She thought about telling her those little teeth in her mouth looked like Tic Tacs or that she was going to call her Two Scoops because of all the raisins on her face, but Alma held her tongue.

"Someone got mugged in my building last night. I didn't sleep a wink," she confessed.

"This neighborhood isn't what it used to be. I remember when Malcolm X used to walk the streets preaching black unity and how he even inspired the junkies to gather around," Joy said. "They would be nodding out at his speeches and trying to pick people's pockets at the same time."

"The only thing you can do nowadays is carry you some of this pepper spray. This stuff will send the demons running for cover," Magdalena said.

"Where do I get me some?" Alma asked.

Magdalena reached into her tan leather handbag and handed Alma a fresh can.

"You can keep that on your keychain, and don't be afraid to use it. It won't kill anyone, but it will make them wish they was dead."

"How much do I owe you?" Alma asked, reaching for her purse.

"That's a gift. My son is a police officer, and this is what they use to control criminals. I have a box of that stuff at my house."

Touched, Alma thanked her.

"It's a pleasure. No one should be scared to live in their own home," Magdalena said. Alma was glad she hadn't mentioned the raisins to Two Scoops.

chapter eight

Alma felt self-conscious being the only woman standing in the crowded ballroom without a red hat on. The room looked like a bed of spring geraniums. In addition, she knew the smell of her perfume couldn't cover up the thick menthol odor of the Bengay she'd had to rub on her back to loosen up the muscles from her fall. She wondered how long it would take for the giant purple-black bruise to fade. It had been three weeks now, and it still hurt like hell. The Epsom salt baths didn't help a bit. It was the price of getting old, as was her annoyance at the loud music the DJ was playing.

This is young people music. These women are too damn

old to be dancing to rap songs. Alma was ready to go, but as she turned to leave, Sisters Dee, Magdalena, and Joy approached carrying drinks.

"What's up, girl?" Joy yelled. "You look more nervous than a whore in church."

"This isn't my kind of music," Alma said.

Drunk and with two drinks, Joy offered one to Alma.

"Drink this, and you will be on that dance floor screaming, 'Drop it like it's hot! Drop it like it's hot!'"

"What's in it?" Alma asked cautiously.

"It's easier to tell you what's not in it," she joked.

Alma sipped the drink.

"Don't sip it! Drank it! Take it to the head," Joy said, raising her glass.

"I'm a lady. I like to sip and savor whatever I drink," Alma said.

"To each his own," Joy said, then bravely gulped the firewater with the girls.

Alma took a big sip, not wanting to be a party pooper. "Wow, you weren't lying! That's strong!"

"The good news is that from this point on, the rest of them will taste like nothing but good," Magdalena said.

They all laughed in agreement. It didn't take long for the drink to hit Alma. She instantly felt warm all over and found herself nodding her head to the rap music. *This is going to be fun.*

"Someone stinks," Joy said angrily. "This is why I hate coming to these functions. Somebody always got to show up smelling like Bengay. If your ass is that old, keep it home. Right?"

The Red Hats all agreed. Alma wanted to disappear. She was pleased when a rather handsome and dapper man interrupted their conversation.

"Hello, ladies."

"Hi, James," Joy said nervously.

"Who is this?" he asked, focusing on Alma.

"My name is Alma."

"Hello, pretty Miss Alma. My name is James Debron, and it is so nice to meet you."

Alma shook his hand. James gently kissed it. Alma snatched her hand away.

"I don't bite, unless you ask me to," James said slyly. "May I have this dance?"

"I don't like this music. Maybe later," Alma said.

"You promise?"

"I said later."

James smiled, glanced at his watch, then glided back into the crowd. Alma didn't know what had happened, but she felt dizzy. She blamed the alcohol.

"I need to sit down," she told Dee.

James had been outside smoking a Hoya Double Corona Cuban cigar when he spied Alma in the midst of all the Red Hats. He noticed she was the only woman there not wearing the red and purple.

Sixty-eight years old and happily single made James a regular at the Red Hat parties. Born into a tribe of five sisters created a need for women to validate him. He loved to flirt but hardly ever pursued the romances, because he realized that if he gave in to one, then he couldn't flirt freely with all the rest of them. He was also very discreet about his rendezvous, learning from his sisters that women hated men who kiss and tell.

Another reason he curbed his sexual appetite with these women was the money he generated in his family law practice from the Red Hats. They trusted him, and any indiscretion would compromise that. James didn't mix business with pleasure, which allowed him to see past Alma's façade.

The sparkle in her eye called his soul. He decided then and there that he would make it his business to bring her heart pleasure.

Sister Dee and Alma sat at a table watching the other girls dance in front of them.

"My biggest problem right now isn't my diabetes, it's knowing that my daughter lives three blocks away from me and refuses to visit. She'll walk right by me at the supermarket and not even speak. That hurts more than any disease you could ever have," Dee said drunkenly. "This is a picture of her. That's my Kelly."

Alma looked at the photo of an attractive young mulatto woman dressed in a high school cap and gown. The picture answered all of Alma's questions about Delilah's easiness around black folks. Alma felt her guard drop as she looked Dee in her pain-filled eyes.

"She's a pretty girl," Alma offered.

As she looked up, Alma made eye contact with James, who was smiling at her from across the room. She pretended not to see him, but he knew otherwise. He let her off the hook and turned away first.

"I mean, I don't even know what I did to her to make her treat me so bad. I told her about my condition, and all she did was shrug her shoulders and say, 'What do you want me to do?'"

"I would have slapped the taste out of her mouth," Alma said. "My kids aren't perfect, but they know they'd better fake it around me. Time-outs don't work with black children. You got to beat their ass when they don't give you any other option."

The music stopped.

"Ladies and gentlemen, we have a special request going out to a young lady named Alma from James. James said to let you know he paid me a lot of money to play this song, so you'd better dance with him," the DJ joked.

The crowd parted as James smoothly waltzed over to Alma's table. She stood up to run, but he was light on his feet and caught her before she could find the exit sign with her eyes.

"It's *later,*" he said cockily.

James took her hand and reassured her with his eyes that he would be gentle. Alma grabbed her drink from the table and guzzled it. James smiled as they walked onto the dance floor. She was nervous, but he pulled her close and moved rhythmically, side to side, his hand on her waist guiding her with the control of a great lover. Alma had to fight the images in her head. It had been a long time since she was this intimate with a man. She felt as if James was able to read her mind by the way he looked into her eyes. She decided to close them to prevent him from reading her heart.

The DJ must have read her mind, too, because he changed the song to something more up-tempo. James didn't miss a beat. He quickly adapted his moves to the beat of the song.

Boy, this man sure can dance, Alma thought as she tried to keep up. It didn't take long for her to shake out the cobwebs. After all, she had won many dance contests as a young woman with Harold. Alma had a few moves of her own that she threw at James. He allowed her to show-case her stuff, then responded with a slightly competitive display of his own choreography. The Red Hats gathered around to watch them go at it.

"Get down, Alma! Show him what you got, girl," they chimed in.

After five songs, James decided to call it quits. The entire ballroom applauded as they made their way off the floor.

"Can I get you a drink, Alma?" James offered.

"Sure. That would be nice."

As she watched James step to the bar, Alma felt self-conscious and guilty. It was as if the whole room and Harold were watching her act the fool.

When James returned with two apple martinis in his hands, Alma was gone.

"Where did she go?" he asked Dee.

"She got an emergency call and had to leave. She told me to be sure to tell you what a good time she had with you."

"That's so strange," he said still searching the room for her.

"Are you going to drink both of those martinis?" Joy asked. Before James could answer, she relieved him of one of the frosted glasses.

It took two cups of muddy black coffee to help lift the dark cloud over Alma's head. She hadn't had a hangover in many years and vowed never to have one again if she could only rid herself of this one. Alma was amazed that the other women at the table were so talkative and unaffected by the alcohol they had inhaled last night.

Dee opened an assortment of medicine bottles and arranged a colorful mound of pills on the table before her.

"You're going to take all of those?" Alma asked.

"Yeah. This one is for my sugar, and this one is to help with my blood. These two help the nausea from taking these two, and the other three are vitamins. I'm all messed up. But you do what you have to do to survive."

"You should stop eating so many sweets in order to survive, if you ask me."

"Sugar is my weakness. I tried to stop, but life just isn't as sweet without it," Dee said as she forced the pills down her gullet with the aid of a tall, cool glass of water.

"She's been dealing with a lot of stress since her daughter stopped talking to her." Joy leaned in and whispered to Alma. "That little wench won't even let her see her own grandchild. Be easy on her."

"I can't be somebody's friend if I can't tell the truth," Alma said loudly enough for everyone to hear. "If you really cared about her, you'd be saying the same thing instead of whispering in my ear for me to be quiet."

"So what happened with you and James last night?" Magdalena changed the subject.

"Nothing. We danced, that's all."

"He was looking for you all night. You must have really put it on him, girl. James can have any woman he wants. That man is a real catch," Joy offered. "Any woman in her right mind would be happy to let him into her world."

"Well, I must not be in my right mind, because I know his kind. He's nothing but a womanizer who thinks he can charm his way up under any skirt he likes. I'm not interested. I know a dog when I see one, even when it's not on a leash."

"Well, do me a favor and send him my way," Joy added.

"You can have him. It's too soon for me to be thinking about a man."

"Are you divorced?" Joy pried.

"Whatever I am is none of your business. It's just too soon. Let's leave it at that."

"It's never too soon for me. I'm tired of my rabbit," Joy complained. "That thing is going to hop away from me I use it so much," she finished.

"I think the girls are just trying to say don't let a good one get away. James is a good man. He lost his wife a while ago," Dee offered, "and he isn't as bad as he comes off. Just lonely, that's all. And we all know lonely."

"Speaking of which, we've got something for you," Magdalena said.

"Me?"

Dee reached under the table and produced a hatbox. She placed it in front of Alma.

"I can't . . ."

"Just open it. You can't say no if you don't even know what it is." Dee pushed the box toward Alma.

Alma opened the box and pulled out a beautiful, large-brimmed, red-feathered hat accented with gorgeous strawberry-red brocade.

"Welcome to the Red Hats," the women said in chorus.

"It's beautiful, but I can't accept it."

"Why not?" Joy asked.

"Because I don't want to be a part of no damn cult!" Alma exploded.

"What makes you think we are a cult?" Dee asked.

"You walk alike, talk alike, and dress alike. If that isn't the signs of a cult, I don't know what is. Besides, if I wanted to join the Red Hats, I would have asked to join. I don't like anything being forced on me. You don't know me. I don't need this!"

Alma stood and tossed her money onto the table.

"That's for my coffee. Just stay away from me, OK?"

"Alma, we give hats to all those who are special to us. We're just trying to be your friends," Dee tried to explain.

"I don't need no more damn friends! I pick my friends, they don't pick me. Y'all keep that red hat, I don't want it."

Alma hurried out of the café, leaving the Red Hats dumbfounded.

chapter nine

Alma couldn't stay inside another minute and decided to take a walk in the park. The leaves were gone, and it was unusually cold. She enjoyed it nonetheless, at least until she saw Bob and Seymour playing a game of chess. They raised their heads to see her and give each other a look but did not speak. She didn't speak, either. But she felt slighted. How dare they? The least they could do was show some respect on the strength of their friendship with Harold. But neither had been welcomed in her house for the longest. Why did she care now?

When she entered the building, she noticed something different: the light was out in the hallway. Her heart began to beat faster, and not just because of the stairs. She was digging down in her purse for the door keys when she heard a voice.

"Hello, young lady," a male voice said.

Alma didn't give the words time to reach her ears before she started spraying the man in the face with her pepper spray. The man howled in pain.

"My eyes! Oh, my God, Alma, I can't see!"

Alma recognized the man flailing about in front of her. It was James Debron.

"James! Is that you?" she asked.

"Yes, what is wrong with you, woman?"

"What's wrong with you, sneaking up on me like that?"

"I can't see. It's burning!" he cried. "I need to wash my eyes."

"OK."

Alma opened the door and pulled James inside. She took him by the hand and led him to the kitchen. She turned the cold water on and leaned him over the sink.

"Hang on."

She went to the bathroom and came back with a handful of face cloths. They seemed to stay there for the longest, splashing water in his face. After a while, he sighed and pulled back from the sink. Alma stepped back and watched, wondering if he was going to cuss her out or something. She noticed how nicely he was dressed and how the water was soaking the front of his shirt and messing up his nice cashmere jacket. She'd noticed how soft it was as she was trying to get him positioned to rinse his eyes. Her stomach was in knots.

James opened his eyes and looked at her. He shook his head and smiled.

"Now, what are you smiling for? I nearly put your eyes out. I'm sorry, but you scared the daylights out of me."

"You're beautiful, even as a blur."

She felt her face turn hot and her emotions go haywire. "What are you doing here? How'd you know where I live?"

James patted his pocket, as if he remembered something. He pulled out a glove. "You dropped this at the dance, and I wanted to return it to you."

Alma reached for the glove recalling that, yes, it had been missing.

"Who gave you my address? Dee?"

"No, Dee didn't. She wouldn't. She said you were private. I used to be a lawyer. I have contacts in the police department. I'm sorry, I should have called."

"Yes, you should've. I'm a married woman and—" She stopped in mid-sentence, feeling awkward about what she was saying. She stood up and gestured toward the door. "You have to go now. I'm really sorry. Thank you for bringing me my glove."

"Thank you for taking care of me, Alma."

Her eyes got big, and she wrung her hands, walking toward the door and reaching for the knob. He straightened his shirt and jacket as best he could and set the face cloth on the dining table.

"Alma, take care of yourself. Listen, I was hoping we could, I could take you to dinner one night, sometime."

"Didn't I tell you? I'm married."

She looked at the floor, then right into his eyes.

"Please." She motioned for the door.

James gave her one last look and smile before walking away. She shut the door and stared at the glove still in her hand. She put it to her nose—it smelled . . . like James.

Winter came fast. The trees were left naked and the ground bald with patches of slush and snow. Alma still spent most of her day at the window, fearful of what the outside had to offer. At night, she read her Bible, seeking comfort and understanding of why life had dealt her such an awful blow. It seemed as if nothing ever stayed the same in her life. There was always something to make life miserable.

Today it was the heater. The radiator had been making loud banging noises for the past week, from not being bled, and all of a sudden, it upped and stopped working. She complained to the building's assistant manager, who claimed there was nothing he could do. He suggested she use the oven to heat the place. What nerve! She went over his head and called the building's owner, threatening to alert the authorities. Again, she was told this was a problem the city had to fix. *The city,* she thought. *Who the hell is the city?* It was too vague for her to figure out.

She spent the day wrapped in a blanket on the phone trying to reach *the city.* Finally, a woman with the electric company explained to Alma that the problem was not the city's and referred her to an agency you call for "got no heat." They told her it was being handled and they should have it fixed within the next few hours. That was ten hours ago.

Alma broke down and turned the oven on to stay warm. It was so cold she could see her breath. She pulled the love seat into the kitchen and set up a nesting place in order to stay warm and rest. Because it was Friday, she feared the problem wouldn't be handled until Monday. City workers were off on weekends, so there wasn't anyone to respond to complaints. To make matters worse, a huge snowstorm was in the forecast.

Alma nodded off to sleep. Her subconscious dream state told her the heat must be back on, because she suddenly felt extremely hot, especially around her feet. It felt so hot it almost burned. Alma started awake, kicking the smoldering blanket from her feet just as the first flames took hold. She must have settled too close to the oven, and the flimsy blanket had caught fire.

The blanket quickly ignited the tablecloth and then the kitchen curtains. Alma screamed for help as she fought to extinguish the flames with an even flimsier blanket. She panicked, seeing the two fires spread quickly. Within thirty seconds, the flames were too intense to put out. She couldn't even reach the sink for water.

Alma freaked out. She backed away, standing in the middle of the living room, screaming for help. Smoke filled the apartment, making it difficult to breathe. Not knowing what else to do, she grabbed the only thing that mattered to her, a framed wedding photo showing a smiling, unknowing Harold and her leather bible.

Run, she heard her mind say.

So she did. Alma ran from the apartment, yelling at the top of her lungs.

"Fire!" Alma banged on every door she passed. "Get out! There's a fire!"

Doors opened, and mothers with children and husbands with wives fled for their lives. Fire engines could be heard in the distance.

Alma huddled outside the building, wrapped in a nice, warm wool blanket Mrs. Johnson had put around her shoulders as she coddled the only things she had left in this world—a bible and a picture in a frame. She was too shocked to cry and more than a little angry, knowing that her apartment was the only one lost to the fire. All her antique dolls gone! She wished she could have stood the pain of the flames so she might have burned in the hell that was before her eyes.

What now? People returned to their apartments. No one asked what she was going to do. They acted as if the inconvenience were all her fault. Where was the neighborly love she read about in the Bible? As she stood there alone, she noticed Bob, Seymour, and Rae Ann standing across the street staring at her. She pleaded for help with her eyes. As if choreographed, they turned in unison and walked away.

A fireman suggested she go to a local shelter and apologized for not being able to give her a ride on the truck because of insurance issues. He was kind enough to give her cab fare and his deepest sympathies for what she was going through. *Thanks a lot.*

Alma felt like a criminal as she stood in line at the downtown shelter. It was worse than the treatment she got at the police station, where the officer hadn't even offered her a cup of coffee. He sat there sipping his own steaming cup as he filled out the police report, not even bothering to look up from the paperwork. Alma thought he was avoiding eye contact for fear he would see his own mother, sister, or daughter in her eyes.

He allowed her to make a few calls to Jesse, who didn't pick up. After leaving numerous messages, she gave up that option. That boy wasn't worth a damn. Where could he be on a cold winter night?

The attendant at the shelter told her she was lucky tonight because they had an opening. It was all Alma could do not to grab the woman and beat her to the ground. *Lucky?* How could she use that word? How insensitive could someone be?

The bed she was given was a hard cot with a dirty, brown, itchy blanket. God only knew where it had been. Alma was careful not to let it touch any bare skin. Lying there amid the smell of urine and cigarettes, Alma allowed tears to fall from her eyes. She didn't care if the woman in the bed next to her listened as she cursed God for putting her through such pain. She felt like Job in the Bible. The prophet whom God had allowed the devil to strip of everything he knew and loved, striking him with a disease of malignant boils from head to toe just to get him to curse his God. In the end, Job proved his faith to the God he professed to love and was healed of the painful boils that afflicted him, then given back everything he had lost tenfold.

"What kind of a God and Father puts his children through all of this?" Alma cried to no one in particular.

"Amen," the woman said as she took a long drag from her cigarette.

"Show your face, you coward! Where is the God who saved everyone else? What happened to the miracle worker?" Alma cried with eyes closed. "Are you just going to let me suffer like this? Is this what I get for believing in you? Help me! God, please help me!"

"Alma!"

Alma opened her eyes to see Sister Dee standing over

her, reaching out to help her up. She was wearing a ruby-red cloche with a matching feather jutting from its narrow brim.

Alma took her hand and stood, then collapsed into her arms.

"I'm sorry I said all those mean things to you. I'm so sorry." She sobbed. "I didn't mean it. I don't know why I say the things I say sometimes."

"It's OK. Let's just get you out of here. This isn't a place for a lady," Dee whispered.

Dee lived in a row house she owned in the Bronx. She rented out three of the four apartments and lived in the two-bedroom on the second floor. It was nicely decorated with antiques that were pieces of art to Alma. She'd always dreamed of having Tiffany lamps and Persian rugs like these. Dee set her up in her daughter's room.

"She never visits anyway, so I'm glad it's finally going to good use. This old brass bed was my grandmother's. You'll sleep well tonight."

"Thank you. Thank you so much."

"You stop thanking me, OK? It's our duty as human beings to look out for one another. It is my joy to be here for you. One day, you may have to return the favor for me," Dee said.

"As God is my witness, I will," Alma promised.

"You go on and take a nice hot bath. I'll bring you one

of my gowns and robes to put on." Alma noticed the hatbox the girls had intended for her sitting on top of a beautiful cherry-wood dresser.

"That's yours, you know," Dee said as she left the room.

Alma stared at the hatbox for a moment, then dismissed the thought of trying the gift on.

Alma soaked in the hot tub for almost an hour, thinking about all she had lost—photos of her children and grandchildren, her dishes, family jewelry, old vinyl records, birth certificates, clothing, identification, bank statements, and her priceless antique dolls. Those were just a few that came to mind. She thought about all of the running around she had to do to get her finances back in order. How would she do that with no proof of who she was?

When she climbed from the tub, Alma noticed how wrinkled her hands and feet were from soaking so long. Dee had knocked several times to check on her. The loaner gown was made from a fine silk that felt good against her skin. Dee brought Alma a warm slice of apple pie with a scoop of vanilla ice cream. She gave herself an injection of insulin so Alma wouldn't have to eat it alone. It was disturbing to see how easily she took the needle, so matter-of-fact. No flinching or crying. She did it as if she were simply picking a piece of lint off her sweater. No big deal.

Alma stared at the needle as Dee placed it on the tiny square alcohol swab now next to her wedding picture.

"Here, sip on this." Dee poured a healthy shot of expensive brandy into a crystal snifter. It warmed Alma's insides right away.

"This is nice," Alma said.

Dee noticed the needle near the picture frame and moved it.

"Sorry."

"It's OK."

"What a handsome couple."

"Thank you."

"You must miss him."

Alma nodded.

"I know that void. I lost my husband, too. Only he didn't die, he ran away from me. Just like my Kelly, he was always running. I was just too blind to see it. Everyone saw it but me. He joined the army right after I got pregnant, so he could travel and see the world. That's what he said. I wanted to see it, too, so I packed up and followed him to Japan. He transferred to Germany, then San Diego, California. It wasn't until he wanted to go to Alaska that I figured out it was me he was trying to shake.

"So I moved back to New York," Dee continued, "and got a job as a social worker, trying to help other women with children out of wedlock."

"What happened between you and your daughter?" Alma asked.

"Kelly blames me for chasing her father away. In her mind, it's my fault she never had a daddy in her life. Maybe she's right. Carl certainly didn't want to be with me. But I still love that man. I send him e-mails and pictures of us sometimes, hoping he will see that I am his one and only true love. I swear I could give up sugar for him."

"Why don't you give it up for *you*?" Alma asked.

"It makes me feel loved."

Alma reached for her picture and held the silver frame to her heart. "I took this man for granted," Alma stated. "I never thought in a million years he would leave me like this. I wish I could have forgiven him. He hurt me so bad."

"How?"

"He slept with my best friend. Donna and I were like sisters. I'd known her since childhood. I told her everything about Harold. She knew he was the world to me, so I trusted her around him." Alma paused for a moment.

"What a fool I was," she continued. Afterward, Harold blamed me for always having her around. Maybe I was naïve to let her sleep over and then leave them alone while I shopped. Hell, the food was for them. I didn't think best friends did such things to each other. Not best friends. I just couldn't forgive him. I wanted to, but I couldn't. I'm bone-tired, Dee. Do you mind if I get some sleep?"

"Sure. Sweet dreams." Dee kissed her forehead and quietly left the room.

Alma felt a heavy weight lifting off her chest after opening up to this stranger. She began to pray: *Heavenly Father,*

I thank you for this day. I don't know what you see in me that you sent this nice lady to save me out of the pit of hell, but I am grateful. Please help me to release this pain and submit to your will, not mine. I can't do it alone, so I beg you to hold my hand and get me to the other side. I thank you in Jesus's name. Amen.

chapter ten

Alma didn't sleep well, because anxiety kept her tossing and turning throughout the night. She got up as soon as the sun started to rise to make breakfast for her gracious hostess. She hated feeling as if she owed somebody something. It was hard to cook in a new environment not knowing where anything was, but Alma was determined to feel that she was earning her keep. She made the easiest thing she could find, which was bacon and eggs with toast, orange juice, and coffee. It wasn't Folgers, but it would do. Dee was pleasantly surprised when she walked into the kitchen, although the smell of the bacon had pulled her from sleep.

"You didn't have to do that, honey."

"It's the least I could do after you've taken me into your home and looked after me like this," Alma said. She watched Dee put nutmeg on her eggs and five sugars in her coffee.

"It's OK. I'll drink a little green tea later to balance out my sugar," Dee explained.

Alma looked down to see a huge, nasty blue bruise on Dee's left foot.

"What happened to your foot?" she asked.

"Oh. I dropped a pot on it a few weeks ago. It takes a while to heal with the diabetes. It'll be all right," Dee told her confidently.

Alma shook her head and decided to change the subject. "Can I borrow an outfit to go downtown? I have to get my identification replaced."

"Certainly."

"And can I borrow a few dollars, too? I'll pay it right back after I talk to one of my children."

"Not to worry. I can give you twenty dollars."

"Not give. Just loan it to me. I will have it back to you no later than tomorrow."

"That's fine," Dee said. "You know, the girls will be coming over this afternoon. You're welcome to join us for tea. I really could use some help."

"Sure, but I have a lot to do today. I've got to stop by the apartment and see if there's anything salvageable and then run all sorts of errands. I won't be back here until the evening. That is, if I can stay another night with you?" Alma asked.

"My house is your house. I will give you a set of keys before you leave. Don't you go feeling like a stranger around me, OK?"

"OK."

Alma made up her mind that she would come back and help out even if she had to endure the embarrassment of all of those Red Hats knowing her misfortune. She knew people liked to see someone down and out just to make them feel better about their own situation in life. Especially Joy—that one was sure a piece of work!

Alma spent half the morning at the insurance agency trying to collect. She had to cuss out two of the workers for insinuating that she was an arsonist. Alma threatened to burn their entire building down if they didn't pay her claim. The manager was called to restore some order. He was very sympathetic and comforted her with a listening ear and a cup of Folgers. When she left, Alma was still angry and not a step closer to payment. Insurance was the biggest scam on the planet.

Alma tried to call Jesse, but that fool still wasn't around. She didn't want to call Angel for fear she would have to go back to live with the Elephant Man. Unfortunately, calling Angel was her only option.

Angel begged her mother to get on a plane and come to stay with her, but Alma passed. All she needed was some money to get her through the transition of finding a new place to live.

Angel sent her seven hundred and fifty dollars by Western Union, and since she didn't have identification, the password was *Nia,* easy for Alma to remember.

Alma went shopping to get a couple of outfits so she wouldn't have to feel like a beggar. She wrote a thank you card to Dee and put in an extra fifty dollars so Dee would know she wasn't going to freeload off her.

As a part of her promise to God to be a better Christian, Alma agreed to help Sister Dee host a little seminar for the Red Hats. They would get together once a month with a lawyer to discuss any legal advice the sisters might need. Dee felt this would be a good opportunity for Alma to get advice regarding her insurance claim. They would serve tea and sandwiches for the ladies and a guest, which was the reason they were now in the supermarket shopping.

"Maybe we should get some pies for a little dessert afterward," Dee said.

"I'm not that big on sweets, and I don't think you should be, either. Let's just get what we came here for. I'm not trying to tell you how to live your life, but I wouldn't feel right if I didn't speak my mind. I'm not going to help you do anything that's bad for you. Sorry, but that's just the way I am," Alma stated.

"You're right, sweets is the last thing I need. My sugar was up to six hundred last night before I finally got to sleep."

"I don't know what that means, but it sounds high."

"Seventy to one hundred fifty is supposed to be normal," Dee confided.

"Hello, ladies!"

Alma looked up to see James standing in front of her with the biggest smile she'd ever seen on a straight man. He smiled so big it made her smile, too.

"You look absolutely beautiful, Alma."

"Thank you," Alma said as she primped her hair, not knowing what else to do with her nervous hands.

"And so do you, Dee."

"Don't lie to me, James! Stevie Wonder could see who you are looking at," Dee joked.

"I'm so sorry to hear about your misfortune," James said to Alma. "I hope and pray that everything works out for you. If there's anything I can do, please don't hesitate to ask."

"Thank you, but God will provide. Dee is taking great care of me right now," Alma said.

"Dee is a wonderful woman. They don't make them like her anymore."

James flashed his million-dollar smile as he carried the ladies' packages home for them. Alma felt a slight bounce in her step as she walked alongside him. She nearly bumped into several parking meters on the way, trying not to get too close to this man who was pulling her out of her comfortable orbit. *What a strong, gentle man*, she thought, as he carried the groceries, climbing the steps with the ease of a gazelle. Dee kept nudging her behind his back, indicating how cute he was. Alma felt like a teenage girl in high school.

When James left, Alma's heart slowed to its normal pace. She tried to be indifferent, but it was hard to pull off. Dee offered her information, knowing that Alma was too proud and private to ask for it.

"You know he lives right across the street from here. You can see his house from my window," Dee confided.

"Really? He's such a flirt. I'm sure he has all the women he can handle. So, what do you want me to make first?" Alma changed the subject.

"You can make the sandwiches, and I'll put on the coffee and boil the water for tea."

Alma's mind was racing with images of James and her dancing together, the smell of the glove, and that smile. Damn, he had a beautiful smile. She stared out at the windows on the buildings across from her, trying to figure out which one was his.

The Red Hats began to arrive. It took only three of them for the place to come alive with laughter and lots of chatter. By the time all twelve of the Red Hats arrived, the place was so loud you could hardly hear the doorbell ringing.

Alma was closest to it and offered to see who was on the other side.

"Hello," said James, who was now dressed in a business suit.

"Look, I don't think it is appropriate for you to be coming by here to pursue me," Alma said sternly.

"Neither do I," James said as he walked past her. "I'm here for the seminar."

"What do you mean?"

"I guess Dee didn't tell you. I'm the lawyer. Don't worry, I'll pursue you some other time."

Alma stood there with the door open, stunned silent.

Damn, I feel stupid. Maybe I should just run out this house and never come back.

"Alma, close that door and come sit down," Dee called.

Alma sat in the back of the room and watched James field questions from the sisters. He was very knowledgeable about the law. She liked how he could solve problems in a split second. It was like watching someone solve a Rubik's Cube. Three twists, and he had it.

Occasionally, he would look in her direction as if he wanted her to offer a problem for him to fix. She didn't know the women well enough to open up like that, and she was really impressed with Dee for not telling these strangers her situation. When asked why she was living there, Dee would say it was "because of none ya," meaning none of your business! Alma saw Joy trying way too hard to get the wrong kind of attention from James. He knew she wanted more than his understanding of the law and didn't play into any of her innuendo. Classy.

The hour passed quickly as James listened, informed, and utterly charmed the Red Hats. He agreed to return at the end of the month to see how their situations turned out. They fed him sandwiches and coffee and packed him some dessert for the road. Alma wondered where the sweets came from. She had fought a hard battle at the supermarket not to buy any. She searched to see who the culprit was, so she could have a conversation with them about Dee's condition and how they could all help her fight the sugar habit.

It made her mad to see Dee with a plate of cherry pie à la mode in her hands. It was weird to see how happy it made her to have sweets. Her eyes rolled back in her head as she took the first bite. It looked orgasmic.

As James was saying his good-byes, Dee grabbed his hand and pulled him over to Alma.

"James, I know you have to go, but I need you to talk to my girlfriend about some legal advice she needs. It's none of my business, so I'm going to let you talk by yourselves." Dee winked at Alma, then turned and walked away, leaving them staring at each other in an awkward silence.

"I'm sorry about earlier. I didn't know."

"No apology needed. It was cute."

"Cute?"

"Yeah. So Alma, how may I be of service to you?"

"Well, you know my placed burned down, right?"

"Yes."

"I had a renter's insurance policy, but I'm having a hard time collecting on it."

"I'll be happy to represent you."

"The thing is, I don't have very much money to pay you. So you have to tell me up front what it is going to cost me."

"Dinner."

"What?"

"It's going to cost you having dinner with me," he said.

"That's it?" Alma asked.

"No. I pick the time and place. Deal?" James extended his hand, and Alma shook it.

"Deal!" she exclaimed.

They matched each other's smile.

The morning of the insurance meeting, Alma had agreed to see James for coffee to discuss the final details of her case. She also had agreed that this did not let her off the hook for dinner. As Alma sat across from James, who had stacks of telephone transcripts, building code information, and various other legal papers in front of him, she found herself suddenly at ease in his company.

He wore a different hat when he was conducting business. No flirting and no million-dollar smile. He was a great listener and wanted to soak it all up. She was embarrassed at having to explain that her husband was deceased after she'd told him she was married. James acted as if he already knew and even expressed his heartfelt sorrow for her loss.

He encouraged her to take him through the night of the fire again, step by step, and asked numerous questions. Did she hear the fire alarm? How close was she to the lighted oven? Did she make calls to the building manager and the heating company regarding the broken pipes? The fact that the building's assistant manager had told her to use the oven caused him to write more notes on his legal pad.

James was finished. After he seemed satisfied with the answers, he told Alma he was confident that not only would she get her money, but if she was up to it, she also had a case against the building owner for not having the fire alarms up to code.

Alma stated that she only wanted what was hers. This seemed to impress James.

When they arrived at the insurance company, Alma was ready to sit through hours of questioning, but James asked her to wait in the reception area while he went into a glassed conference room with a couple of their big-shot attorneys.

Alma didn't hear what was being said, but she noticed how quickly James was able to make the men in the room uncomfortable. He gestured toward her several times, causing the men to look in her direction. It took almost three hours for them to go through all of the documents James produced. Alma was wired from the coffee the receptionist kept bringing her and started to pace, so much so that she had to walk the stairs several times to calm the jitters. After the third journey up and down the six stories, James caught up with her on the stairwell.

"What happened?" she asked.

"They were tough. I had to play the race card, the widow card, and the we-will-sue-you card."

"What did they say?"

"Your check will be in the mail by the end of the week."

Alma screamed for joy, grabbed James, and gave him a big hug. He flashed that million-dollar smile, and she quickly removed her arms from around his waist.

When Alma returned to Dee's place, she was in a terrific mood. Tears were the last thing she expected to encounter. Dee was sitting on the couch, sobbing uncontrollably. An empty pie tin and a few candy wrappers were on the floor around her.

"What's wrong?"

"I went to see Kelly and asked her what I could do to make us better, and she said the only thing I could do for her was to die! How could she say that to her mother? What did I ever do so wrong to make her hate me like this?" Dee wept.

"I learned that children only treat you with respect if you demand it from them. She sounds as if she needs some discipline."

"I know. Her father used to tell me to spank her, but I couldn't bring myself to do it because we spent so much time together. I wanted her to love me. She hates me!"

"Dee, why are you sweating so much?" Alma asked with concern.

"Maybe it's from eating too much sugar. I don't feel well. My head is spinning, Alma. Please stop the room from spinning."

Dee's eyes began to roll up, revealing the whites. Her body started to shake violently. When she spewed them both with partly digested pecan pie, Alma knew it was time to call the hospital.

"Send someone right away, and we need an ambulance."

It took only seven minutes for the cops and ambulance to arrive. Alma made sure they moved quickly. She climbed into the ambulance and went with them to the hospital after collecting Dee's purse with all of her personal information.

Alma was pleasantly surprised to see a few of the Red Hats had beaten them to the hospital and alerted the doctors that Dee was on her way. They were very organized, which impressed Alma. She was confident that she had gotten this same tender loving care when the Red Hats found her after her attempted suicide.

Alma said her own silent prayer as Magdalena held hands with twenty-six Red Hats and prayed loudly in the waiting area for Dee's return to health. It was too showy for her to hold hands like that. It felt forced. After about two hours, the doctor approached the group to explain Dee's condition.

"She's going to be OK. We had to amputate her left foot because the gangrene was spreading up the leg."

"You what?" Alma demanded. "Who gave you permission to do that? Did you ask her if that's what she wanted?"

"I'm sorry, but we did what we had to do. She will recover completely," the doctor said.

"You don't recover completely when your left foot has been cut off against your will!" Alma shouted.

The doctor turned and walked away. Alma was furious. Joy rubbed her back and told her to calm down. Alma gave her a look that must have sent chills down the spines of all twenty-six Red Hats. Alma stormed out of the emergency room.

chapter eleven

Alma walked with purpose behind a young woman with the hood of her down jacket drawn tightly about her face. A winter mist blew out of both of their mouths as they climbed the steps leading into the tenement building. Alma allowed her to make it into the entrance doorway first.

"Are you Kelly?" Alma asked sweetly.

"Who are you?" the young woman asked.

"My name is not important. I'm here to tell you your mother is in the hospital."

"Good," Kelly said as she attempted to put her key in the lock.

"It's not good. She needs to see you."

"Too bad," Kelly replied coldly.

Alma snatched her keys from her hands.

"You need to come with me right now," Alma demanded.

"I don't want to see that bitch!"

"That bitch, as you call her, loves you. But the one standing in front of you don't give a damn about you. Now, if you don't get your disrespectful narrow ass down them stairs and into that cab, I will pick you up and drag you there."

"You must be crazy, old lady," Kelly accused.

"That's what they tell me," Alma replied.

Alma set her bag down on the ground in preparation for the battle to come.

"So what's it gonna be?" Alma taunted.

The women squared off and went at it, tooth and nail.

Alma showed up at Dee's hospital room bruised, bleeding from a scratch on the face, and alone.

"What happened to you?" Magdalena asked.

"I had to handle some business. How's she doing?" Alma asked.

"Not too good," Magdalena whispered. "She keeps slipping in and out of consciousness."

Alma took Dee's hand. "Hey, Dee, it's Alma."

"Alma? Is that you? I'm sorry. I'm so sorry."

"You don't have nothing to be sorry about," Alma told her.

"They took my foot off. I can't do anything with one foot. I can't do this." Dee cried softly.

"You won't have to do it alone. You have an army of Red Hats behind you."

Dee shook her head as if to say that was not enough.

"I brought someone to see you."

"Who?"

"Get in here!" Alma shouted to the doorway. Dee turned to see Kelly enter, bruised up and in more disarray than Alma. The Red Hats were in shock. Dee smiled through her tears.

"Come on, ladies, let's give them some alone time," Alma ordered. She gave Kelly one final threatening look to remind her she had better be nice as she followed the Red Hats from the room.

Alma had the place spotlessly clean for Dee's arrival. It was an honor to dust and clean the beautiful woodwork and her antiques. She took the liberty of throwing away anything in the kitchen that had sugar in it and replacing it with a healthy alternative. She visited several holistic doctors and bought all kinds of books on curing the sugar habit.

She was grateful her insurance check had come so quickly. It meant she could find her own place now and not have to be a burden on Sister Dee. Alma decided she would stay until Dee could get up on her feet—or foot now. There would be many life changes ahead for her new friend, and Alma felt a need to be there to help her through some of those challenging times. After all, she wouldn't be alive if it had not been for that woman.

Receiving the insurance check had also made her think about James. She was a little disappointed that he had yet to ask her on that date. She had spotted him in his brownstone the other day. He'd waved, but she didn't want him to think she was stalking him, so she'd pretended she hadn't seen him. Maybe she should have at least waved back before shutting the blinds on him and cutting off all the lights.

Kelly and a couple of Red Hats brought Dee home in a wheelchair. There was a beautiful basket of pink roses sitting on her lap.

"Welcome home." Alma gave her a big hug and kiss.

"Thank you, Alma."

"Thank me for what?"

"For everything, especially for bringing my Kelly back to me. I don't know what you said to her, but she is a whole new person."

"Oh, I just threatened to cut her with my butcher knife, that's all."

Everyone laughed, except Kelly.

"Here, these roses are for you," Dee said.

"You didn't have to do that."

"I didn't. They're from James. And there's a card with them."

Alma hid her excitement as she read the invitation to dinner at a secret location that weekend. He said he would send a car to pick her up and reminded her to bring her dancing shoes.

Alma wheeled Dee's chair to her favorite spot in the park and sat on the bench overlooking the lake. Dee sipped unsweetened tea while Alma enjoyed a cup of Folgers from Harold's battered thermos, which she'd found among the ruins of her apartment fire. They were both too occupied with their own fears to feel the cold of the winter morning.

"Well, today is the big day," Dee said.

"What big day?"

"Your date with James, silly."

"I'm not going."

"What? You've got to be kidding me!" Dee exclaimed.

"I need you to do me a favor and tell him I can't make it."

"I will do no such thing. What are you scared of, Alma? I told you, James is a good man."

"Well, I'm not such a good woman," Alma replied. "I'll just hurt him. You don't know me."

"I don't think *you* know you," Dee said. "The Alma I know is a sweet, caring, and very giving woman. You need to be that way with yourself. It's OK to let people in, you know. Not everyone wants to hurt you. I look at myself right now, and I don't know if I'll ever be able to walk again. But I know for sure that I won't be able to walk if I don't try. You got to try, Alma. Let people in."

"I can't."

"You can."

"I feel so bad inside."

"Well, you have to let it out. Just let it go."

"How do you let go with what I've done?"

"You have to believe that God forgives in a big way."

"Can God forgive a woman who returned wrong for wrong? I didn't tell you the whole story about Harold and me. You see . . ." She hesitated. "After I found out he slept with my best friend, I wanted to hurt him like he hurt me. So I slept with *his* best friend, too. Then I found out I was pregnant with Seymour's baby, and I was so scared to tell Harold that I thought about performing my own abortion. I just wanted it out of me," Alma said, reliving the horror in her mind.

"Being raised in the church made it impossible for me to go through with that idea, so I lied and told Harold it was his. When Jesse was born, it was obvious from the hazel eyes whose child he was. Harold never said anything out of his own guilt, but I could see he wasn't as affectionate toward little Jesse as he was with the other children. My punishment was that he never cut Seymour off. He kept him as his friend so I'd never forget.

"One day, I got mad at Harold, and I told Jesse that he wasn't his father. I don't know how I let that come out my mouth, but as I was saying it, I saw a change in my son. It devastated him. I used him as a weapon, and I ended up breaking my poor baby's heart. Can God forgive something like that?" Alma asked.

"Yes, God can," Dee said. "The real question is, can Alma forgive herself?"

That night, Alma sat down in front of her wedding picture, pondering what to say. "Harold, we need to talk. Now, I'm about to tell you what my pride wouldn't let me say to you years ago. I'm sorry that I ever looked at you with hate in my eyes, because I know now it was love behind my glare. I wish I could have told you what I needed from you so that you could have rescued me from the hell that I chose. Any other man would have left me as much as I put you through. But you weren't just any other man, and I guess that's why it hurt so bad when you and Donna betrayed me." Alma paused to fight a wave of hurt that the memory brought back.

"I want to thank you for loving me even though I wasn't lovable. I just pray that you can forgive me, Harold. I've decided that I'm going to move on with my life now. I met someone. He kind of reminds me of you. Maybe this is God's way of giving me a second chance. When we meet up in paradise, I'll let you know how it turned out. I love you, Harold. Always have. Always will. Rest well, my sweet has-been."

Alma stood, fanned out her black dress with the red bow around the waist, and exited the room.

Dee was in the living room eating celery sticks when Alma entered wearing her vibrant red hat.

"Do you mind if I borrow this?" Alma asked.

"I told you, it's yours."

"Thank you. I will always wear it with pride."

Sister Dee watched as Alma walked out of the building with a bounce in her step, into the waiting limousine.

The chauffer held the door open wide enough for Alma to get a glimpse of James's smile beaming from within the long black symbol of elegance. As she took her seat at his side, Alma let out a sigh of relief, and joy mixed with pure excitement. When she inhaled the smell of James, it pleased her senses.

"Hello, gorgeous," James whispered. "Beautiful does not describe what I see before me."

Alma blushed as she played with the buttons on the arm console. "You don't look too bad yourself. So, where are we headed?"

"Can I enjoy this magnificent view first?" James replied.

"We've got all night for you to see anything you want."

"Anything?"

"Yes, anything with clothes on it," Alma cautioned.

James laughed slyly as if she didn't fully understand his power to seduce. "Driver, take us to Smith and Wollensky at Forty-ninth and Third," James ordered.

"It's hot in here. Is the heat on?" Alma blurted out.

James checked the heat indicator above his head. "It

says seventy-two degrees. Is that too high for you? Wait a minute." He leaned over Alma and turned the seat heater off. "You accidentally turned the seat heater on."

Alma felt something quiver between her legs as he leaned into her airspace. She was grateful for the invention of panties, because they caught what only God and she knew James's touch elicited from her.

"Excuse me."

Alma wondered if he had done that on purpose because of the way he looked at her as he moved back to his own seat. Alma looked out the window, thinking about how good it felt to know she was still capable of being aroused without even a touch. It had been a long time . . . too long. She felt James's hungry stare, and the thought of it made her quiver again.

"Are you OK?"

"I'm fine. Can you put on some music, please?"

James skipped through the music menu with the satellite radio controller above their heads. Alma enjoyed how he knew his way around the car. The light from the vanity mirror gave him a mysterious glow as he concentrated on finding the perfect score for the ride. He quickly zipped past a classical station, then briefly paused to listen to a little modern jazz. As if reading Alma's mind, he continued until he found the oldies but goodies that please the ears of any music lover. "Fly Me to the Moon" was the song that played.

James sang along in a low, raspy voice. He wasn't a good

singer, but he sure sounded good to Alma, who joined in to calm her racing heart.

"Now, that's good music!" James exclaimed when the song ended. "I don't know what these kids today think they're singing, but it isn't anything like this."

Alma nodded in agreement, then turned to look out the window to avoid his spell for a moment. She thought about how beautiful the city was at night as they glided down the West Side Highway looking over to the Jersey skyline. She was happy to be out and promised herself that she was going to stop fighting and just enjoy every moment of this night.

She recognized the green sign with the white background as they pulled up to Smith and Wollensky. This was a place where she had always wanted to dine, but she and Harold could never afford it. The greeter was very friendly and had their table ready as soon as they entered. She saw James surreptitiously place a bill in his hand before he departed. James picked a 2006 bottle of Caymus cabernet sauvignon. He sniffed then sipped a small amount and explained to Alma that when this special-selection wine opened up, she would be able to taste plenty of intense flavors such as black currant, cherry, mocha, and a pepper spice.

"Will it give me a buzz? Because that's all I care about," she joked.

"That's my job," James said.

"Oh, really?"

"Yes. Don't you feel it yet?"

"No," Alma lied.

"OK, then I'm going to have to turn on my high beams."

Alma crossed her legs to quiet her libido, then lifted her glass to his toast.

"To the wonder of life. And the joy of you being in mine."

"I'll drink to that."

Alma mimicked the way James did his tasting before enjoying a sip of wine.

"Wow, this is good. So, tell me how a man with good looks and great taste in wine, food, and clothing isn't already off the market?"

"I haven't found the woman who meets all of my needs yet," James said.

Alma gave him a questioning look that said, *What kind of needs do you have?*

"Let me explain that. I was married for twenty-three of the most beautiful years of my life to a woman who loved me so hard I didn't think I deserved it. Every day was special. She took care of me and my six children and never had an unkind word to say about it. We never argued. Not to say we didn't disagree a lot, but Nadia would simply say, 'Let's try it your way first.' Most of the time, we would do it her way because I was too afraid to be wrong. And ninety-nine point nine percent of the time, she was right."

"Where is she now?" Alma asked.

"She died. And so did a part of me. I was single for

two years, then I tried to get back in the game. I hated it. Trying to pretend you're interested in someone you know in your heart isn't the one is a sad place to be. I even lived with a woman for a year, lying to her and myself that it was going somewhere, until I got the courage to be alone again. Nadia set the bar too high for me to settle for just anyone."

Alma didn't know if it was the wine she was feeling or if it was the sincerity of James's confession that had her so connected to him. The waiter arrived with a tray of prime uncooked selections of beef. James ordered the porterhouse for himself and the ribeye for Alma, stating that it would be more flavorful than his choice. The waiter refilled their glasses, then faded out of view.

"How did she die?"

"Diabetes. That's how I met the Red Hats. One day, I walked into the clinic with Nadia and saw all these women in their red hats and purple dresses gathered to support Delilah. I thought I had walked into a church revival. They all came to the funeral and took care of the reception for me. I was so grateful to them, because I was just a shell of a man. I truly needed them at that time."

"Was Joy one of the women you dated?" Alma asked, trying her best to not sound insecure.

"Yes. But Joy is trouble. She was a mistake."

"Is that who you lived with?"

"No. I lived with a woman named Megan."

"Megan? That sounds like a white girl."

"She was white," James confessed.

That's two strikes against you, Alma noted to herself. *How could you betray the race that way?* She thought about Todd and his white wife, her stringy hair entangled in her hairbrush. *Why would you want that in your bed?*

"Are you all right?" James asked.

"I'm fine," Alma lied.

"Yes, you sure are fine."

Alma forced a smile to her face, accepting the compliment. As if on cue, the waiter returned to fill her glass of cabernet. When the steaks arrived, they were cooked to perfection. Not pink on the inside, just the way Alma liked it. She hardly spoke through the rest of the dinner. A few nods and "Oh, reallys" to look interested, but her mind was trying to accept Joy and the white woman. The soufflé put the dinner over the top. The melted chocolate in the middle was orgasmic when chased by the homemade vanilla ice cream. Alma laughed to herself at the thought that chocolate and vanilla got along so well together on the plate. She felt a little embarrassed by the amount she ate. Glasses of port wine magically appeared to seal the buzz in for the night. The thick and sweet liquid was so smooth it made her notice the corners of James's lips and the way they begged to be kissed by her. She excused herself and went to the restroom to sort out her conflicting emotions.

Calm yourself, girl, Alma told her reflection in the bathroom mirror. *You don't even know this man, and you're thinking about kissing and God knows what else you want to do to him.*

It didn't help that a woman entered the bathroom shortly after her and said, "That's a beautiful man you're with."

You can have him came to Alma's mind, but her mouth refused to say it. She thanked the woman instead. After dabbing her face with a cold hand towel, Alma made her way back to the table, where James sat tracing his finger around the wine label the waiter had extracted and sealed between two pieces of cellophane. She hoped she didn't look as high as she felt.

"What's that for?"

"Memories. You may never want to see me again, and at least I'll have this to remind me of the wonderful time I had with you."

Back in the limousine, Etta James was singing "Trust in Me."

The limousine was directed to the West Village. They were both disappointed by the headliners playing at both the Vanguard and the Blue Note, so Alma agreed to ride down to Battery Park City and take a walk. Alma was warm on the inside from the alcohol, but she had goose bumps on her arms from the cold winter air, so James draped his handsome black wool jacket over her shoulders. She appreciated his gentlemanly qualities.

"Look at the stars!" Alma exclaimed as they strolled along the walkway. "I haven't seen stars in so long I forgot they existed."

"So did I, until I saw you."

"Why do you always say things like that?"

"Like what?" James asked.

"The compliments. You never stop."

"The way to a man's heart is through his stomach, and the way to a woman's heart is through her ears."

"Who told you that?"

"My mother."

"Well, I'm not going say your mother lied, but not all women want to hear sweet nothings."

"I'd rather kiss you instead."

Before Alma could reply, his mouth was against hers. The slightest moan forced its way out of her soul. When she opened her eyes, he was staring back at her with a smile that said, *I got you!* And he was right. She tasted that dessert again on his lips and went back for seconds and thirds.

When they pulled up to Sister Dee's building, Alma was sad the night was ending. She wished she could kiss some more.

"I had a great time with you," she said.

"So did I."

"May I kiss you?" Alma asked.

"Anytime and anywhere you want."

"Here, now, and right on those sweet lips," Alma said as she leaned in and softly kissed him. Neither of them closed their eyes.

"Good night, Alma."

"Good night, James."

chapter twelve

Three days passed, and not a word from or sighting of James was tearing Alma up on the inside. Although he didn't have her new cell phone number, he certainly knew where she was staying, which was directly across the street from his building. Alma found a bit of solace in the fact that she had only kissed him and had fought her primal urges to go all the way. Had she done what her body begged her to do and this was his reaction, Alma would have surely borrowed one of Dee's butcher knives and marched over there and carved a piece of dark meat out of him. Not a big piece, just a little something to remember her by. Alma was so deeply disappointed because the night after their date, she had dreamed they had gotten married in front of a room full of Red Hats. Alma was also grateful for her belief in keeping her business to herself and not retelling the night to Sister Dee as she had requested when Alma returned with her face flushed and lipstick smeared unknowingly across her lips.

"It was nice," was all she had said to Dee as she walked past her wheelchair parked in front of the door as Alma entered the apartment.

"I couldn't sleep," Dee had confessed.

I will, Alma had thought as she made them both some hot chamomile tea. But she hadn't. She'd called Angel to relay every minute detail to her. Darryl had been shocked when he picked up the phone at two A.M.

"Hello, it's Alma. Could you please put Angel on the phone, sweetie?"

"Your crazy mother is on the phone," she heard him say to Angel.

Alma had decided on day two of no James "Missing in Action" Debron that she would start looking for her own place to live. As she walked around Harlem, where she felt the rent would be most reasonable, images of James kept popping into her head. How could he say all those sweet things to her and not mean them? What kind of cruel game did he like to play?

When I do see him, I'm going to walk right past him as if he's invisible, Alma had convinced herself as she walked toward her building on the opposite side of her street. His side.

She was thrilled on the third day of grieving when Sister Dee invited her to go to Atlantic City for a weekend of fun and games with the Red Hats.

Any kind of game would be better than the one she was now being forced to play by Mr. Debron. That was her new name for him, Mr. Debron. And Mr. Debron would have no more power over her from this point on. It was supposed to be a three-day trip. Dee suggested she pack something to party in, too. They were going to stay at the Trump Plaza Hotel, where the Red Hats got an amazing group deal.

The girls gathered at Dee's place. The van, complete with a hydraulic lift for Dee's wheelchair, was waiting at the curb. Alma was helping out in the kitchen, making healthy snacks for their three-plus-hour trip, when out of the corner of her eye, she caught a glimpse of James emerging from his cave. He wore a long beige wool coat with earmuffs under a brown fedora and what looked like mittens on his hands. It was a bit overdone for the cool winter day. A lighter jacket would have sufficed, Alma thought. James looked up at the window for a moment, as if contemplating coming over to their building, then suddenly turned and walked eastward toward the supermarket. Alma was sure that he didn't see her since she was standing by the stove.

"I'll be back shortly, ladies," Alma announced as she grabbed her coat and maxi-length sweater and headed for the door.

"Hurry up, Alma, everyone is here and ready to go," Dee said.

Alma didn't hear anything except the voice in her head that wanted some kind of closure with James. She was determined to run into him accidentally and give him a piece of her mind. She wished she were younger so she could jump down the steps a little faster and catch up to him before he disappeared to God knows where. Her instincts said he was supermarket bound, so she went the back way so as not to have to run behind him. She was correct. James was standing in line holding two cans of chicken noodle soup, an orange juice, and some crackers. He looked happy to see her enter the market.

"Hey, Alma," he called in a hoarse whisper, waving to her from across the store.

Alma waved back, mostly out of embarrassment. She picked up her basket and proceeded to shop for the nothing she'd come to buy. When she got to the produce aisle, he was behind her. Alma smelled his cologne before he even opened his mouth. It wasn't strong, it was just seared into her memory bank, and the slight whiff made her turn around to see if she was right.

"I'm sorry I didn't call or come by," he said.

"You don't owe me any apologies. We're grown folks," Alma lied.

"Yes, I do," he insisted. "I've been very sick for the past few days. This is my first day out of the house."

Alma searched his glassy eyes and knew instantly from

the raspiness of his voice that he was telling the truth. She knew that sick look from being up late at night nursing her children back to health.

"Well, if you eat that nasty canned soup, it's just going to make you feel sicker. Go put that stuff away. I'll make you some of my famous chicken noodle soup. Go on before I change my mind."

James flashed a grateful smile and hurried off as fast as he could to return the items he was about to purchase. Alma began picking out fresh vegetables and herbs. When James returned, she had garlic, onions, celery, carrots, potatoes, ginger, cilantro, and lemons in her basket. They walked together to buy the chicken pieces and pasta noodles, then headed out. Alma was on a mission to fix this man.

"Excuse the mess," James said as they entered his place.

Alma was impressed with his taste. It wasn't the mess he said it was at all. The thing that stood out, besides the mahogany wood floors and expensive contemporary furniture, were several pictures of a beautiful woman in various frames and a giant oil painting of the same woman hanging over the fireplace.

"That's Nadia."

"She's beautiful," Alma said out loud, as if confessing to herself.

"Yes, she was," James said proudly. "The kitchen is this way."

Alma followed him with her feet, but her eyes didn't

leave the painting until she rounded the corner of the entry to a chef's paradise. It was a large kitchen with a chopping table in the center as an island. Copper pots hung overhead, and the Viking stove and other appliances were like something out of a magazine.

"I like to cook, and I need space to move around. Hope you like it."

"I love it," Alma said.

She removed her sweater and coat. James hung them in the entryway closet. After washing her hands, Alma began soaking the chopping vegetables.

"Do you mind if I watch?"

"If you want," she replied. She thought, *You'd better watch.* "Let me make you a drink first. Where's your brandy?"

"In the bar by the pool table."

She put the teapot on and went out into the family room to get the bottle of Fundador sitting on a shelf next to a crystal bottle of Louis XIV. As she headed back into the kitchen, there was that painting again. Nadia had eyes that haunted her. They seemed to smile as if she hadn't a care in the world. How could anyone be that happy? The teapot got her attention as it started a slow, low whistle. Alma made James a hot toddy with some Lipton tea, a tablespoon of honey, half of a lemon, and the best ingredient of all, two ounces of Fundador.

"That's good. I may need another one of these."

"I'll make you another after you eat your soup."

"Yes, Miss Alma."

The soup simmered, and all of Alma's ill feelings toward the invalid James disappeared. They smiled at each other like high school lovers every time Alma looked up from her culinary duties.

"Oh, my God, I'm supposed to be going away with the girls!" she suddenly remembered. "I have to run and tell them I can't make it."

"I can take it from here. You go be with your friends."

"Nonsense. I'll be right back."

She left without her sweater so she'd have an excuse to come back.

"I'm so sorry, Dee, but I'm not going to be able to ride with you. I'll catch a bus later and meet y'all at the Trump."

"What's so important that you can't ride with us?" Joy snapped.

"First of all, I was talking to Dee. And second, it is none of your damn business who and what I have to do," Alma warned.

Joy rolled her eyes and allowed a *humph* sound to escape from her mouth to save face, but she also saw that Alma was not to be taken lightly.

"I'll be in the van," Joy announced before walking out of the apartment.

"I didn't mean to disrespect your house, Dee, but that woman does not sit well with me."

"I understand. You go take care of whatever you have to handle, and we will see you there. I'll research the bus to take online and write down the schedule for you. It will be right on the table by the door," Dee said.

Joy was standing by the van smoking a cigarette as Alma walked across the street toward James's building. Alma rang the bell, then gave her a territorial look as the door buzzed open and she entered.

James sat at his table like a child as Alma served him the soup.

"My sinuses are blocked, but I can still see how good this looks."

"That soup is going to clear all that up. I put a lot of fresh ginger and cayenne pepper in there. I hope you have some tissue handy."

"I got a brand-new handkerchief right here," he said proudly, holding it up for her approval.

"Good. Hold on one second while I put the final touch on it."

Alma cut a lemon in half, then squeezed it into the soup. A bit of it squirted into James's eye.

"Owch. You don't like my eyes, huh, Alma?" he said jokingly.

"I love your eyes. I'm sorry." Alma dabbed his eye, then kissed it gently. "Better?"

"I think some got into the other eye, too." Alma kissed the other eye. James held her by the waist, and she pulled his head into her breasts. "Now I'm better."

Alma sat across from him as he devoured the soup.

"You're right about clearing out my sinuses. Man, this soup is amazing!" he said while wiping his nose with the handkerchief.

Alma smiled, then got up to make the second hot toddy she had promised. She put in a little extra Fundador to help break up the congestion she heard in his cough. They sat in the living room as he drank it from the steaming mug. Alma noticed the sweat it created on the bridge of his nose.

"I feel bad about taking your jacket that night. It's all my fault."

"You just made it worth it. Thank you, Alma," James said as he stretched out on the couch. Within five minutes, he was knocked out.

Alma found a blanket and a pillow in his bedroom. She propped him up and covered him to his neck, kissed his forehead, and started to tiptoe out the door. She heard him mumbling a protest but ignored his drunken request for her to stay the night with him.

chapter thirteen

On the bus to Atlantic City, Alma felt really good about herself. She had forgotten how simple it was to please a man. A little kindness was all it took. She used to be like that with Harold. What did he do to make her resent doing what came so naturally for her? Old feelings of anger started to rise, and then the thought of James's shiny eyes smiling up at her from the couch instantly calmed the rage that tried to rear its ugly head. Alma took a deep breath and promised herself she would try to replace unhappy Harold memories with James's sweet nothings.

Two hours into the trip on the ancient Greyhound bus, Alma felt nauseated from the toxic smell oozing from the bathroom's blue sanitizer water. She decided to change the fragrance in the rolling coffin. Using her hatbox as a dinner tray, Alma enjoyed a snack of fried chicken and potato salad. The other passengers looked on in envy as she devoured the perfectly seasoned feast before their hungry eyes. After she was done eating and licking the residue from her fingers, she dusted the crumbs off the hatbox, read a few chapters out of her Bible, then took a nap.

As the bus pulled up to the Trump, Alma saw a frail older woman in a red hat being helped out of a car by a handsome young man who was the spitting image of his mother holding on to his arm. Several of the other Red Hats were there to greet the woman. They all wore their big hats like proud peacocks. Alma didn't understand how these women could wear those loud hats out in public all the time. She felt too embarrassed to put hers on without a purpose, especially now that she had worn it on her date with James. The hat had taken on a more romantic quality for her. When Alma stepped off the bus, Magdalena started screaming like a teenager at a high school football game.

"Alma! Hey, girl!" Magdalena yelled. It was obvious that she had a couple of those free casino drinks in her system.

"Hi, Magdalena," Alma said, lowering her voice in hopes of letting Magdalena know that it was OK to speak at human decibels.

"Did you just get in?"

"You see me getting off this bus?"

"I'm sorry. Those Long Islands are strong. Do you know that you can walk around outside with liquor here?"

"I don't think you should walk around with any more tonight."

"Girl, you are hilarious," Magdalena answered. "Come on, let's get you checked in. I think you're staying next door to Joy."

"Oh, great," Alma said under her breath.

Magdalena grabbed her by the arm and started to pull her toward the front door.

"Wait. I want you to meet Stacy." Magdalena stopped suddenly, then pulled Alma toward the older woman with her son. "Stacy, this is Alma. She is one of us."

"Hello, honey. You sure are pretty," the woman said.

"Thank you, Stacy."

Alma noticed that the woman's head shook like the plastic dog on the dashboard of a low rider's car. Stacy's hands trembled to match the constant movement of her head.

"This is my son Kenny. He is such a big helper to me. I couldn't do anything without my Kenny."

"Nice to meet you, ma'am," Kenny said with a slight bow as he shook Alma's hand.

Stacy looked up from the ground and saw Alma smiling at her. "Hello, honey. You sure are pretty," she said again.

"She got Alzheimer's," Magdalena whispered. "She'll do that all night long. Let's get out of here before she sees you again. I don't know why Sister Dee always invites this kooky old broad to our girls' nights out."

* * *

Alma was annoyed as soon as she stepped into her less-than-average accommodations. Next door, Joy had her television blasting some new-school R&B music and was singing along with the nasty woman singing the song about going down to meet and play with the one eyed monster. She decided to change her room in order to avoid confrontation, but as she picked up the phone, the other line rang.

"We're going to meet for dinner at Roberto's in thirty minutes. It's in the center of the hotel after the atrium," Dee said.

"I want to change my room."

"Can it wait? We had a hard time getting the reservation for fifteen."

"OK, Dee," Alma replied.

She listened to the squealing coming from next door as she hung up the phone, regretting the decision.

Roberto's was a nice Italian restaurant decorated with Old World flair. The red-and-white-checkered tablecloths added to the nostalgic feel. Alma had two seats to choose from at the table. One was directly across from Stacy, and the other was an empty chair right next to Joy, who was on her third drink. Alma chose to sit across from the kook. As soon as Stacy saw her settle in, she smiled.

"Hello, honey. You sure are pretty."

"Thank you, Stacy. I like your hat. It's lovely," Alma said, hoping to change the channel.

"My son bought it for me." Stacy beamed.

"Well, he's got great taste. I'm sure you are very proud."

"Do you have any children?"

"Yes, I have three, two boys and one girl." Alma beamed back.

She was relieved to know that Stacy could do more than say "Hello, honey." She decided to keep probing to keep Stacy engaged.

"So, what got you into the Red Hats?"

"I retired, then realized that I didn't have any friends. My Kenny recommended I join the Red Hats. Kenny is my son."

"Yes, I met him earlier."

"Hey, Stacy, there goes Magdalena!" Joy shouted from the other end of the table.

"Hello, honey. You sure are pretty," Stacy said to Magdalena.

"And there goes Sister Dee," Joy said mockingly.

Stacy turned to Sister Dee and smiled. "Hello, honey. You sure are pretty."

Joy almost fell over laughing.

"That's not nice," Dee reprimanded.

"It may not be nice, but it sure is funny. Hey, Stacy, there goes Alma," Joy said through her laughter.

"That's enough of this," Alma said as she stood up. "Don't put me in your sick little game. I don't appreciate it, and I certainly don't find it funny."

"Oh, sit down, Alma. I always do this," Joy said.

"So, you're always an asshole? Is that what you're saying?"

Stacy and the rest of the Red Hats laughed.

"Bitch, I'm tired of your attitude. Ever since we met, I noticed you had a thing against me," Joy snapped back as she stood with a fire of hate in her eyes.

"Ladies, please!" Sister Dee said as she positioned her wheelchair between the two angry women.

"It's a long fall to the ground. Don't make me show you the way. I'm not the one, Joy. If I fight you, I promise I will kill you. They'll be no pulling hair, scratching eyes, or kicking and biting. I'm just going to take this fork and stab you in your throat. That's the only way I know how to fight," Alma said as she picked up the fork in front of her.

Joy sobered up quickly as the severity of Alma's threat sank in.

"Now, I suggest you apologize to Miss Stacy and sit your ass down so we can enjoy our meal."

"I'm sorry, Stacy," Joy said after swallowing her pride.

Alma sat back down as if nothing had happened. Joy stormed out of Roberto's, sucking her teeth like a hurt little child.

"Thank you," Stacy said, patting Alma's hand.

"I'm sorry about Joy," Dee said apologetically. "We're all happy you joined us. I didn't think you would make it."

"I gave my word. I always honor my word," Alma said.

The rest of the dinner was fun. The tension had left

with Joy. They chatted and laughed until the restaurant began to empty.

"Let's hit the casino. I feel lucky tonight!" Magdalena shouted.

The noise from the slot machines and the smoke from cigars and cigarettes were enough to make Alma want to go to her room. Magdalena begged her to hang out with her at the blackjack tables. Alma agreed to spend an hour with the Red Hats in the casino. Knowing that she had only brought a couple hundred dollars to gamble with, Alma decided to hit the twenty-five-cent slot machines. She sat next to Stacy, who attached herself to her new protector and just stared at the money gobbler in front of her.

"I like the slot machines, because you get your money right away when you win. I don't like having to go cash in my chips. They know that most people end up gambling away their winnings on their way to cash out. I like the sound of my quarters shaking in the plastic cup," Stacy confided as she shook the big cup filled with change.

"Personally, I hate giving my money away," Alma said. "First of all, I can't afford to, and second, I never got over being hustled at a three-card monte table as a teenager. I had a job cleaning movie theaters, and my father made me contribute half of my twenty-two-dollar salary to the house for room and board. He said it was to teach me how the real world works. Nothing in life is free. Anyway, I cashed my first paycheck and was heading to the department store to buy a pair of shoes I had on layaway when I saw these men flipping cards and giving away money to whoever could pick out the red card. There was a giant crowd gathered around the cardboard table, and I kept guessing the right card before they turned it over. There was a young woman standing next to me, and she told me I should play a hand because I was good at this. The man in charge overheard us talking and convinced me to put down ten dollars on the red card, because ten would get me twenty, and twenty would get me forty dollars. He was smooth, too. Had the voice of a Holy Ghost preacher. I couldn't resist the temptation he set before me, so I put ten dollars down on what I just knew in my heart was that red card. When he turned it over and it was black, I nearly had a heart attack. Someone yelled "Police!" and the man folded up his table, then everybody took off running except me. I was too devastated to move. When I got home, I told my father what had happened. Daddy shook his head and told me that gambling is a sucker's game. That's why it's called a gamble. It made me feel better thinking that he was sympathetic to my plight. Then Daddy stood up and said, 'Go give your mother her eleven dollars for room and board.' He walked away without even looking back to see my tears streaming down my face. After that day, I've never been able to enjoy gambling, because if I lose a penny, I get that same sickening feeling in my stomach. I always bring money to gamble, but I can never get up the courage to play a hand."

"That's one hell of a lesson for a child to learn, but look how it paid off for you," Stacy said. "It probably saved you a ton of money over the years."

"I'm sure you're right. There's been plenty of times when we were so strapped for cash I probably would have tried my hand at the god of luck to dig our way out of financial problems."

Stacy smiled up at Alma. She braced herself for another memory lapse from her new best friend, but it didn't come.

"Can I tell you a secret, Alma?"

"If you really want to."

"My Alzheimer's is not as bad is I make it out to be."

"You mean it's all an act?"

"Oh, no, I really have the disease, but I'm just in the infancy stages of it."

"Then why would you pretend like that?"

"I'm testing out these women. I want to see what they are really about before I commit to joining them. I don't trust many people, Alma. My background didn't help me to build trust in people."

"So, what makes you think you can trust me?" Alma asked.

"The way you stood up for me. It was a genuine reaction to injustice. I used to be a diplomat. I traveled the world fighting injustice and selling the dream of a universal family. I had that same righteous indignation that you showed.

What I learned over the years is that it only takes one person to corrupt the minds of many to do wrong. But it takes many to change the mind of a corrupt person to do right."

"Why did you leave that job?"

"They wanted me to become a spy. My superiors said I had a natural gift of deception. They said I was a chameleon and wanted me to spy on my own government people. I declined and was forced to resign. I still believe in the concept of a universal family. I just don't know if it's with the Red Hats."

"Well, I can't speak for all of them, but I can tell you this for sure, Sister Dee is a good woman. She saved my life. Literally. I owe her more than I can ever repay. So, if she thinks there is some good in Joy and the rest of these other women, then I'm not one to argue with her. I, too, promised myself that I would wait and see what happens before I accept an official label as a Red Hat."

"Damn!" Magdalena yelled angrily as she lost another hand at the blackjack table.

"Let's go get her before she loses everything she owns on the first night," Alma said.

Stacy held her hand as they joined Magdalena at the blackjack table. A fresh glass of red wine from the casino waitress quickly replaced a half-empty one sitting on the edge of the table.

"Are you ready to go yet?" Alma asked.

"Not yet," Magdalena barked without even looking up.

"Let me see what you working with." Alma reached for

the cards and accidentally on purpose spilled the red wine all over Magdalena's yellow blouse.

"Oh, damn, Alma!"

"I'm so sorry. Come on up to my room, and I'll give you one of my new tops. I am so very sorry," Alma repeated.

Magdalena grabbed her chips and purse, then stumbled toward the elevator, supported by Alma and Stacy.

"Let me just lay my head down for a minute," Magdalena begged after changing her top in Alma's room.

Within thirty seconds, Magdalena was out cold. She snored like a big black bear in the middle of winter. Alma and Stacy shook their heads in unison at the sad sight of Magdalena sprawled out on the small bed.

"Come on, let me walk you to your room, Stacy."

"I'm OK, sweetheart. I can certainly find my way."

"I wouldn't feel right if your Alzheimer's kicked in for real and you got lost in this big hotel. You're on my watch right now. Besides, I'm not going to be able to sleep with all that snoring going on in here."

Alma took Stacy by the hand and brought her to her room. Kenny was there to let Stacy in.

"What a nice young man you are," Alma commented. "I thought you had left your mother behind with the Red Hats."

"No, ma'am. Wherever my mother goes, I go," Kenny said.

"You just stay in the room until she comes back?" Alma asked.

"Yes, ma'am. She took care of me when I needed it, and now it's my turn to take care of her. Right, Momma?"

Stacy beamed as she nodded yes.

On her way back through the casino, Alma got a phone call. She was not used to the ring tone of the new cell phone, so at first she thought it was one of the slot machines announcing a winner. The loud techno sound followed her until she looked into her bag and checked the caller ID. It was James.

"Hello, beautiful. Did I catch you at a bad time?" he asked.

"Not really. I was just about to call it a night. What are you doing up so late?"

"I ran out of your soup and your smiles and was wondering when I can get some more from you."

Damn, he had a way with words.

"I should be home in two days."

"That feels like forever. I may get sick again waiting on my cure to come home."

Alma took a seat by the elevators for fear of getting cut off from him in the steel box. "Trust me, you'll be fine."

"How's Atlantic City treating you? How much money have you won?"

"Talking to you is the gamble."

"No, baby, I'm a sure bet. And together we will both win."

"I like the way that sounds."

Alma sat there talking on the phone for an hour. His voice serenaded her heart. Knowing there was someone on this planet who thought she was special made her feel special. Her phone felt a little hot in her hand, so Alma kept switching ears, hoping the radiation wouldn't kill her in the middle of her conversation with James. It wasn't until the battery warning beeped that she allowed herself to let him go.

"My phone is dying, James."

"So will I if I don't see you in two days. Hurry home, Alma."

"I will. Good night, James."

"Good night, sweet Alma."

She held the heated phone to her breast and looked up to heaven, silently thanking God for this wonderful man he had brought into her life.

chapter fourteen

Alma awakened with a stiff neck from sleeping in the chair. Magdalena lay spread-eagle the entire night, taking up all of the bed and all of the air in the room with her grizzly-bear snore. Her breasts hung to the sides from lifting her bra to scratch her big sweaty titties.

"Magdalena, wake up. It's six o'clock in the morning and time for you to go," Alma said.

Magdalena woke mid-snore. "Oh, God, my head is killing me. Where am I?"

"You're in my room. I couldn't get you to move over, so I had to sleep in this chair."

"What time is it?"

" 'I'm sorry' is supposed to be the words coming out of your mouth," Alma scolded. "How about a 'Thank you for your kindness, Alma'?"

"I'm sorry."

"And?"

"And thank you," Magdalena said unconvincingly. "Damn. Stop giving me grief. I just woke up. I'm still drunk."

"You're going to have to leave now. I am in no mood to teach a grown woman manners. You take your big drunk ass out my room right now. I need to get some sleep."

Magdalena sucked her teeth and mumbled something incoherent as she stumbled out of the room, still drunk from the night before. Alma let the door slam behind her. A second later, there was a knock at the door.

"Who is it?"

"Maggie. I left my room key in there."

"Too bad. If you wouldn't have been such an ingrate, I might have slipped it to you under the door. But you go on downstairs and get a new key from the front desk," Alma said from behind the locked door.

"Alma!"

"If you don't get from in front of my door, I'm going to call security."

Magdalena kicked the door, then headed for the elevators. Alma laughed to herself, thinking about how tore up Magdalena probably looked as she stumbled down the hallway.

* * *

When Alma finally woke up, it was twelve thirty in the afternoon. She hadn't slept that late in years. It felt as if she got cheated out of half the day. She made herself a cup of coffee with the little coffee maker on the bathroom sink. She hated the powdered cream but couldn't drink her coffee black. Alma called Dee's room.

"Hello."

"Hey, it's Alma. Are you dressed yet?"

"Yes. I've been up since nine watching the news."

"Can I treat you to lunch?" Alma asked.

"There's a nice all-you-can-eat buffet downstairs. I can call the girls and have them meet us there."

"I'd rather take just you someplace special."

"If you're treating, I'm eating," Dee joked.

Alma pushed Dee's wheelchair down the Atlantic City Boardwalk as they strolled toward the Tropicana Hotel where the Palm restaurant was housed. Dee had wanted to try their famous Gigi salad and ribeye steak. Alma didn't like the looks she got from some of the black women who visibly questioned her role in Dee's life. The looks said, *You must be the caretaker or the maid.* She knew those stares from way back. The funny thing was, Sister Dee didn't even notice them. She just kept talking and pointing out everything that caught her eye.

When they were finally seated in the restaurant, Alma realized that her appetite had been worked up from pushing the metal chair seven city blocks. She ordered the porterhouse with mashed potatoes and creamed spinach. Dee ordered what she'd come for, the Gigi and ribeye.

"Thank you so much for lunch, Alma."

"I've been wanting to do something nice for you ever since you took me in. I'm not used to letting people do things for me. It goes against my upbringing."

"The truth is, you have been a godsend for me. I don't know how I would have made it after my operation if it weren't for you taking care of me like you do. All the cooking, cleaning, and most of all, just your company. I know you had planned on leaving a while ago, but I'm sure thankful you let me talk you into staying."

Dee took out her kit and tested her blood-sugar level.

"Oh, dear. It's three-sixteen. That's high."

"How did it get so high? Aren't you watching what you eat?"

Dee's silence said everything. She looked like a child who'd been caught trying to steal a cookie out of the jar. Her eyes welled up.

"Dee, what's the matter?"

"It's so hard, Alma. I can't control this disease. I love my sweets too much. Everywhere I go, it's there. My room has a mini-bar. I ate everything in it. I ordered room service three times. Only desserts. I'm like a junkie. What am

I going to do? I can't keep living like this. I look down at my missing foot, and it makes me so depressed that the only thing to make me feel better is some chocolate. Sometimes I wish they'd cut the other one off just so it would match. Jesus, this thing is going to kill me."

"Not if you don't want to die, it won't. You just have to choose living. Where there is life, there is hope, Dee. I know from experience. Six months ago, I wanted out. I couldn't see the next day. Hell, I couldn't see the next minute. I was suffocating and just wanted to be free. Free not to exist. Then you found me and helped me see that tomorrow can be a better day, and there are people in this world who share your pain and sorrows. I'm grateful to you because I can breathe now. I'm starting to taste life again. If I would have given up, I would have never had you as a friend, and I would have never met James."

"I knew it!" Dee exclaimed. "You two will make a great couple."

"I'm not thinking that far ahead. I'm just saying we have to fight for tomorrow, because it's not promised. You have to do things today so that you are prepared to enjoy tomorrow if you're blessed enough to get one."

"You're right. It's just a hard habit to break. It's like smoking cigarettes."

"Cancer cures smoking. Let diabetes cure your sugar cravings."

"Amen to that. I'm going to write it on the refrigerator," Dee said.

They toasted with their water glasses as the food arrived.

"Alma, I'm really not one to get into people's business, but I think you should know that Joy and James used to date at one time."

"I know. He told me. And the fact that I didn't stick that fork in the side of her head yesterday tells me that I'm OK with it. He is entitled to a past. Everybody has one. I have one, too."

"Well, I'm happy to hear that, because I wouldn't feel right knowing I'm keeping a secret from you. I have enough on my mind as it is. I don't need any more drama in my life."

Alma reached across the table and held Dee's hand. "Neither do I," she confessed.

The Red Hats met in the lobby of the hotel at eleven thirty on the dot. They had all donned their red hats. People took pictures as they made their way through the casino like a flock of wild red geese. Alma pushed Dee to make sure she lagged behind Joy, who blazed the trail toward the Spank nightclub on the far side of the casino. Stacy held her son's arm as if she were his prom date. They all sat at a reserved booth in the VIP section of the Spank, which was actually right by the dance floor. Bottles of champagne, vodka, and tequila sat on the table in front of them, compliments of the manager, whose mother was a member of a different chapter of Red Hats back in California. He thanked them for helping his mother find excitement in her old age.

Alma watched Joy down two shots of Patrón like a sailor. She didn't even use the lemon or the salt, just took it to the head, letting out a defiant yell to signify that she was there to let it all hang out.

"The cougar is on the prowl," Joy growled.

The other girls laughed, then took turns downing shots of the firewater.

"Come on, girls! Let's find us some of that fresh young meat."

The Red Hats picked up a glass of champagne each and hit the dance floor. Alma didn't partake. She made up her mind to keep Dee company.

"Oh, my goodness. Joy got herself one," Dee said, gesturing over Alma's shoulder.

Alma turned to see Joy grinding up against a man half her age on the dance floor. The guy sensed her loneliness and began dry-humping her from the back. After a few minutes of this, Joy turned around and kissed him deeply to let him know that tonight she would take it wherever he wanted to go. The young man answered her invitation by lifting her by her ass and spinning her around the crowded dance floor.

"God bless her heart," Alma said, shaking her head like a disappointed parent.

"Poor thing doesn't know how bad she looks right now," Dee said.

"Shoot me if I ever get that desperate. You have my permission. Just take me out of my misery."

"To tell you the truth, Alma, I wish someone would pick me up and spin me around like that," Dee said sadly.

"He'd have to be really strong to lift that wheelchair," Alma joked.

"You are too much." Dee laughed, dodging her self-pity.

Alma watched Magdalena slip out of the club and head for the craps tables in the casino. *She's got a serious problem,* Alma thought as she poured herself and Dee glasses of lemon water.

Stacy was on the dance floor, cutting a rug with Kenny. It was so cute to see them having genuine fun together.

"She raised that young man correctly," Dee said, pointing.

Alma thought about her own sons and couldn't remember them ever dancing together. In fact, they hadn't gone on a lunch or dinner date since they were children. She fought the jealousy that was coming up with a hopeful thought of a call from James later tonight. Joy found her way back to the table to refresh her drink and to wet the young man's whistle. She lifted the vodka bottle and poured a healthy stream into her victim's mouth. Alma shook her head but held her tongue for fear she would look jealous.

"Hello, baby girl," the young prey said to Alma after wiping his mouth with the sleeve of his shirt. "What's your name, Momma?"

"Momma!" Alma answered directly, cutting his flirt off at the pass.

"Why you so mean?" he asked.

"Leave her alone, Charles. She ain't no fun," Joy said.

"Maybe we should bring her back to your place and teach her how to play. You want to play with us?" he asked.

"Joy, take your disrespectful boy toy away from here before there's nothing left but his teeth on the dance floor," Alma threatened. "You know I don't play."

Joy grabbed the vodka bottle and her plaything and led him away from the impending dental-reconstruction work.

Alma felt better after she got out of the shower. The cigarette smell was gone from her skin and hair. She sat on the bed in her room and reached for the remote control, then noticed that the message light was blinking on her cell phone.

"Hey, Miss Wonderful, this is your neighborhood stalker checking in on you. I'm sorry you're not there to talk. It's late here, and I'm about to get some sleep. I was thinking about you. I'm sure I'll see you in my dreams again. If you see me in yours, come sit down and talk to me. If you're not too afraid, give me a kiss, then sit back and let me dream my dream. I miss you. Kisses." James blew a soft kiss.

Alma smiled as she stored the message. There was a

loud noise from someone being thrown against the wall next door. Alma heard giggling, then another thud.

"Oh, God! Yes! Yes!" Joy exclaimed.

Alma turned off her lights and listened to the sounds of Joy getting her groove back. It wasn't just sex. It was a show. It was wild, uninhibited, loud, wake-up-the-neighborhood sex. Alma knew Joy was putting a little extra on it to let her know it was going down in the other room. It worked. Alma felt jealous. She wondered if James could make her scream like that. *It's been a while*, she thought. When it did happen, she was going to wake up the entire planet.

chapter fifteen

Alma helped Kenny escort Stacy to their car, while the other Red Hats get Dee and her wheelchair into the van. It was quite comical to see these old women doing heavy lifting. The chair got bumped around several times before it finally made its way safely in.

"Thank you, ladies," Alma heard Dee say to the group.

"Well, it certainly was a pleasure getting to know you, Alma," Stacy said. "Please take my number, and call me if you ever need a favor. I still have some great connections in some very high places." She winked as she handed Alma her government-sealed business card.

"I will," Alma replied. "Kenny, you keep taking care of her. You only get one mother in this world."

"Yes, ma'am," Kenny said as he carefully closed the passenger door. "My mother really likes you," he whispered. "She doesn't like too many people, so consider it a compliment, and don't hesitate to call her if you ever need a favor or a friend. Good-bye, Miss Alma."

Alma stepped back as the town car pulled out of the parking lot. Stacy turned to give a little wave good-bye to the girls in the van and then a special smile and wave to Alma.

"What are we waiting on?" Alma asked as she settled into her seat in the back of the van next to Dee.

"Joy," the Red Hats said in unison.

"She loves to make an entrance," Magdalena blurted out sarcastically.

A few minutes later, Joy waltzed out of the Trump arm in arm with the young stud. They tongue-kissed each other sloppily. Joy tucked a few dollars into the palm of his hand. He gave her a final swat on the ass and went back into the casino.

"I hope y'all haven't been waiting on me long." Joy giggled.

"Long enough," Magdalena said jealously.

"Sorry, but Charles and I couldn't get enough of each other. I'm sure we kept Alma up all night long. Huh, Alma?"

"You sure did. I hope you used protection. God only knows what these young boys are carrying around these days," Alma said calmly.

"Of course I did."

"You did? Or he did?"

Joy sank silently into her seat with a troubled look on her face.

"Of course she didn't," Magdalena said. "Joy is just plain ol' nasty."

"Well, at least I get some use out of mine. Unlike the rest of you old hags in here," Joy snapped.

"Ladies, please let's not ruin a great trip," Dee interjected.

"Sorry, Sister Dee. I wasn't talking about you."

"Yes, you were, and it's OK with me. It's hard to do it in a wheelchair. Not too many men want to give it to a footless grandmother. I'll bet that's not on anybody's wild-and-crazy-fetish list."

The women all laughed.

"Girl, you are crazy!" Magdalena said, coughing from laughing so hard.

An hour into the ride home, Magdalena turned to face Alma, who was the only other person awake.

"Alma, can I borrow a couple hundred dollars from you? I have to pay my rent when I get back," she whispered.

"You should have thought about that when you was at the blackjack table."

"I did. That's why I was gambling. My Social Security check didn't come last month, and I had to dip into my savings to help out a friend."

"Sounds like you need to call that friend and tell them you need a friend right now."

"Come on, Alma, stop playing."

"I'm not playing. I don't know how you can fix your face to ask me for a handout when you don't even know me."

"You owe me."

"How do you figure that?"

"When you tried to kill your fool self, I was the one who carried your ass down all those steps so you could get some fresh air. None of these other bitches lifted a finger. Except Joy."

Alma was stabbed to the heart. She wanted to jump over the seats and strangle Magdalena's fat neck. Instead, she coolly opened her purse and extracted the two hundred dollars she had planned to gamble with.

"You saved me, now I'm going to save you. We're even. That means if you ever bring up something so painful again, I swear, it's going to be a sad day for the Red Hats." Alma dropped the money into her lap.

"I'm sorry, Alma."

"You sure are, Magdalena."

Alma watched her snatch up the neatly folded money, then turned her attention to the scenic view out the van's window. She tried to calm her angry mind with images of James, but they kept getting replaced with a replay of the events over the past few days with the Red Hats. Stacy was right, Alma thought. These were just lonely, catty women with more bad than good about them. Except for Joy? Why would Joy help carry her down four flights of stairs and then treat her with such contempt?

She would tell Sister Dee to remove her from their activities when they returned. Again, she thought of Stacy and her beautiful smile and those mistrusting eyes. Then she felt a smile on her own lips as she remembered the love and affection Kenny showed his mother. Alma fell asleep thinking about Kenny. He turned into her son Jesse for some reason. Jesse was standing in a building with a gun in his hand. It was silver, a .38 snubnose, like the cops in old movies used to have. He kept playing Russian roulette with the gun. Spinning the barrel to make a clicking sound, then lifting the shiny metal life taker to his temple. He looked down from the window and smiled at Alma, then pulled the trigger.

"No!" she yelled up to him.

Jesse nodded yes. "It's your fault, Momma," he said, before repeating the death wish.

This happened three times, and then suddenly, a little boy holding a shiny horn appeared next to Alma.

"What's he doing?" he asked her innocently.

"He's gambling, baby," she replied, looking down. Then Alma heard the gun go off. *Pow!* She looked to see Jesse fall to the ground at her feet. The little boy disappeared as Alma went to Jesse's aid. She held her son as the life force left his body. She ordered her brain to let her wake up. In her mind, she was aware that it was only a dream, but as she woke from what felt like a drug-induced coma, there were tears rolling down her cheeks.

"Are you all right, Alma?" Dee asked.

Alma saw that all of the women in the van were staring at her. She wiped the tears from her face. "I'm fine. Had a bad dream, that's all."

The rest of the ride was the longest and most uncomfortable trip of Alma's life. Boy, she couldn't wait to get home.

God, make this bad feeling go away, Alma said in a silent prayer.

As they pulled up to the brownstone, Alma saw James sitting on his stoop, holding a small bouquet of flowers.

Thank you, Jesus, Alma thought as she returned James's wave.

He waited patiently as the Red Hats said their good-byes. When the last of them had pulled away in the taxi, James made his way over to Alma and Dee.

"Hello, my sweet," James said after planting a quick, soft kiss on Alma's lips. "These are for you."

"Thank you," she said, sniffing the small bouquet of delicate pink and purple carnations, asters, and Monte Cassinos.

Dee watched them get lost in each other's gaze for a moment. "If you can pull yourselves away from the forces of nature for just one moment and help me get into the building, I would certainly appreciate it."

"I'm sorry, Sister Dee," James said as he grabbed the handles of the wheelchair and pushed her up the building's ramp without taking his eyes off Alma's. They held hands behind Dee as they rode up the tiny elevator. As the door opened, Alma's heart dropped. Jesse was standing there, sweating like the crack fiend he'd become.

"Momma? I need help, Momma. Please help me. I just need a few dollars. I know you said to stay away from you, but I'm really doin' bad right now. Please!" Jesse begged.

"Boy, if you don't get your behind out of here this instant, I will hurt you. Do you hear me?"

"I'm doing bad, Momma. They threw me out of my place because they said I stole some stuff from my neighbor. I didn't take it, Momma. I didn't even know he had a flat-screen. They're lying on me."

"You are embarrassing me. Go on, Get out of here! Now, Jesse!" Alma yelled.

"Where am I supposed to go, huh? You think it's just that easy? You're my mother. You're supposed to take care of me."

Jesse slid down the wall and began to cry. Alma did the same, except she stood over him.

"Do you mind if I talk to him?" James asked.

"Just tell him to go. I don't want to see him like that."

James nodded. Dee took out her house keys and opened the apartment door. Alma followed her inside.

James slid down the wall next to Jesse.

"She hates me!" Jesse cried.

"No mother hates her child, son."

"Why does she treat me like this?"

"Maybe she's disappointed by some of the choices you've made."

"Who are you? Her boyfriend or something?"

"I'm her man friend. Maybe I can be your friend, too."

"Can you loan me some money, friend?"

"No, but I have a few things you can do around my house to earn a few bucks."

"Like what?"

"Let's take a walk and talk about it." James helped Jesse to his feet. "James," he said, extending his hand. "What's your name, young man?"

"Jesse."

Alma watched through the peephole as James escorted Jesse into the elevator. She turned to see Dee crying quietly behind her.

"Pathetic, isn't it?" Alma said.

"He needs help, Alma."

"He needs God's help."

"That, too. But he really needs drug counseling. I know someone good. She's a Red Hat. Very discreet."

"Dee, please don't get in my business. I'll ask for help when I need it," Alma said as she walked into her bedroom and closed the door.

James and Alma sat holding hands in silence, staring at the dirty brown river that rippled in front of them. She'd agreed to take a cab ride with him to what he had named their spot by the water. The place they kissed for the first time. As Alma leaned against his shoulder, she wished that he would kiss her to take the burning thoughts of failure out of her mind.

"What did he say to you?" she asked.

"I can't tell you what he said."

"Why not? He's my son."

"If I did, he would never trust me again, and then the dysfunction could only continue. What I can offer you both is a different perspective."

Alma lifted her head from his shoulder and squinted her eyes at him.

"Why are you looking at me like that? I'm just trying to be a friend to both of you."

She softened her glare as she saw the truth of his intentions in his eyes. "I don't know what to do. He needs to get his life together."

James was silent. Alma watched his mind drift to a sad place. "Did you check out on me?" she asked.

"I'm sorry. I was thinking about my oldest brother who passed away years ago. He was a heroin addict and the shame of my parents. Used to come by the neighborhood and get harassed by the kids who threw rocks and bottles at him while he nodded out on the corners. They didn't know that he was my hero. They didn't care that he was an amazing mathematician. He could break down quantum physics so that a second-grader could understand it. He was a brilliant man in so many ways, but he had a broken heart that he tried to fix with drugs. I always thought it was just a phase he was going through and that his intelligence would overrule his addiction. I believed in my soul of souls that he would wake up one day and say, 'OK, let me get it together.' So I didn't do anything to help him. That's my greatest regret in life. I didn't do anything. I left it to him to fix him. What I learned is that people can't do it alone. We need the love and support of those who say they love and support us."

"You don't understand."

"I don't want to understand. That takes too long. I want to help, because I like seeing you happy. That makes me happy, so I will do whatever it takes to make that happen. Life's problems are simple to fix. We complicate them with our own insecurities and fears. If you let me, I will help you through this."

"I'll think about it."

James kissed her forehead, then wrapped his arms around her as she melted into his chest.

chapter sixteen

Several weeks later, Alma found herself in a foul mood. The thought of Jesse showing up at Dee's house was so devastatingly embarrassing, especially with James at her side. Alma used her negative energy to clean up the house. Thus far, the floors were washed and polished with liquid wax, the chandelier in the entryway was dusted, the bathroom was so clean you could perform surgery in it, and all of the antiques were sparkling after being dipped in Tarn-X. She wished the place were bigger, wanting to do more cleaning. She thought about emptying the closets and rearranging the contents but dismissed that, thinking Dee would probably feel she was snooping. That's what she would have concluded, so she let them be.

"Who does he think he is?" Alma said out loud to no one.

Dee had been picked up by Kelly and her grandchild to go have a play date at the amusement center by the piers. Alma declined to tag along, saying that it was better for them to have some quality time as family. Alma also knew that Kelly was definitely not a fan of hers, being as this was the second time Alma had threatened her life to get this play date on the books.

The hard knock at the front door startled Alma. She immediately thought Jesse had returned. She grabbed a frying pan to give him something to remember her by.

"I told you to stay away from me, didn't I?" Alma said, lifting the pot over her head.

She was shocked to see Joy on the other side of the door. Joy screamed for mercy.

"I'm sorry, Alma!" Joy said, weakly lifting her arm to protect her skull. "I need help. Is Sister Dee here?"

Alma lowered the pan to her side, noticing the infirm look in Joy's eyes. "I thought you were someone else. What's wrong with you?"

"I don't know," Joy said, falling into Alma's arms. "I feel very sick."

Alma helped Joy into the living room, setting her gently on the couch.

"My God, you are burning up. How long have you been like this?"

"Two days. I don't know what is wrong with me."

"Well, we are going to find out," Alma said, picking up the phone.

"You don't have to do this," Joy said weakly.

"Oh, hush up. Just because I don't like you don't mean I don't have to take care of you. Now, lay back and let me call this hospital before you change my mind."

"You are something else," Joy said just before she passed out on the couch.

The ambulance came quickly. Alma was grateful that Dee lived in such a nice neighborhood.

James was watching from his window as the medics hoisted Joy into the back of the emergency vehicle. Alma signaled to him not to come down with a slight shake of her head. She liked how they communicated in silence. She was instantly upset with herself for being so distant from him the past few days. Now, she missed him and wished that the Joy factor wasn't present so he could ride along with them to the hospital.

Alma called Dee, who promised to rally the troops and meet them at the hospital. By the time the paperwork was filled out, seven Red Hats were there with flowers, balloons, and loving support. Alma was impressed most by Stacy's presence.

"Hello, honey. You sure are pretty," Stacy said to Alma, giving her a wink and a smile at their inside joke.

"What are you doing here?" Alma asked Stacy.

"I'm a lot like you, Alma. My bark is worse than my bite. I always try to do the right thing. At my age, I'll never know when it may be me lying up in that hospital room. I don't want to be alone. Besides, the good Lord says that when you return kindness for evil, it's like heaping fiery coals upon that person's head. Plus the fact that Dee told me that you were bringing Joy to the hospital, and I thought to myself it sure would be nice to see you again."

Alma gave her a hug. "Aww, that's so sweet."

Five hours later, a doctor approached the noisy and crowded waiting room. It felt like a wedding reception with all of the Red Hats seated and standing around chatting. Several women showed up with food and fresh coffee, understanding that the dispenser in the hospital was sure to make even the strongest of stomachs sick.

"Which one of you ladies is Alma?" the short bespectacled doctor asked.

"I am."

"May I speak with you in private, please?"

"We're sisters. We have no secrets," Magdalena snapped.

"Sorry, I'm just following the request of the patient, Miss. No offense," the doctor politely replied.

He escorted Alma down the hallway and into an empty room.

"What's wrong with her, Doctor?"

"Mrs. Pryor has contracted hepatitis C and a mild case of gonococcus."

"What's gonococcus?"

"It's commonly known as gonorrhea. Which can be treated with cephalosporin or quinalone. However, the hepatitis's severity is determined by her lifestyle. The disease attacks the liver, so modifying her diet and avoiding foods that tax the liver excessively are critical. She has to exercise regularly, abstain from alcohol, and avoid anal sex and multiple partners."

"Hold on, Doctor. This is way too much information for me to handle. I barely know this woman," Alma said.

"That's strange . . . she said you were the only woman she trusted," the doctor replied. "However, if you would like, I can give you a list of things that she must practice and avoid in order to have a productive life. This is a very serious disease if taken lightly. Have a nice day." He walked away as if he were a mechanic talking about an old car engine.

Alma felt sorry for Joy as she sat in the room with her. The tubes of liquids snaking their way into her veins made her look like a science project.

"Alma?"

"Yes, Joy, I'm here."

"Please don't tell the girls about my condition," Joy begged.

"Your business is your business as far as I'm concerned. If you don't tell them, they won't hear it from me."

"Promise?"

"I promise."

"I feel so bad," Joy said as tears rolled down her face onto the pillow propping up her head.

"They gave you antibiotics. You should be feeling better in a few days."

"No, I feel bad about how I've treated you. I guess I'm just jealous. I felt it the day we found you laying there in that gorgeous red dress with all those pretty flowers surrounding you. I swear you looked like something out of a fairy tale. So beautiful, and even though there was a cut on your head, you looked confident, like royalty. It was obvious that it was your choice to leave this world. Everybody wishes they were more like you. We talk about it all the time."

"Why would anyone want to be like me?" Alma asked.

"Because we know you don't need us. You don't need anyone. You're not afraid like the rest of us."

"That's not true," Alma confessed after a brief moment of reflection. "I'm just as afraid and insecure as the next woman. Maybe I don't let it show as much, but trust me, God, I'm scared to death every day I wake up. But I ask myself, 'Alma, is today the day you throw in the towel, or are you ready to fight to enjoy this day?' That's what you need to do, Joy. You have a hard fight ahead of you."

"I know."

"Don't worry, I've got your back."

Knowing the security that came with that commitment, Joy smiled, then reached out, and Alma slowly took her hand. "Thank you," Joy said.

* * *

Alma sat at the kitchen table, thinking about poor Joy and the recompense of her actions. Her life changed in a night of lust. Had it been true love, it still wouldn't be worth the consequences. Depression, anxiety, difficulty concentrating, insomnia, itching, rashes, stomach upsets, headaches, fevers, and body ache were all symptoms of the disease. Joy was experiencing them all. Alma wished she didn't have to keep this secret, especially since Joy needed so much care while she recovered. Her life would never be the same, although the doctor promised the infection would subside after seven days of the ten-day antibiotic cycle.

Alma was physically exhausted from running back and forth to Joy's place in Brooklyn to cook and make sure she took her medication. Alma felt Dee's stare from across the dining table.

"Alma, I know you don't like people to get into your business, but I wouldn't be a friend to you if I didn't say that I can't see for the life of me how you can give so much time and care to a woman you don't like and yet turn away your own son, who obviously needs you right now," Dee blurted out.

The look on her face confirmed to Alma that this was something Dee had been keeping inside for the past week. Dee backed up in her wheelchair as Alma rose from her seat. It wasn't until she dropped the knife and fork onto the table that Dee stopped seeing her life flash before her eyes.

She braced herself for the blow she suspected would come as Alma walked toward her. It never came. The front door opened and then closed behind Alma.

James was surprised to see Alma at his door so early in the morning. She wasn't wearing makeup and had on a housecoat, so he dismissed the thought of an early-morning booty call. The tears that welled up in her eyes said she needed a friend. James took her into his arms, then into his house. He made her a pot of Folgers. She'd turned him on to it and he hadn't been able to drink anything else.

"I want to help—I need to help my son, but I don't know where to start."

"We'll find him, and you tell him that. Tell him you love him and believe that he was put here to be extraordinary. Let Jesse feel your love and support, and he will have no choice but to get the help he needs."

"What if he doesn't?"

"What if he does?"

Alma smiled, acknowledging the concept that positive thinking was going to be the key to success.

The smell of urine and feces was enough to make a garbage man sick in what was the third crack house she and James searched through looking for Jesse. Shadows of crackheads, both young and old, moved in the darkness.

Alma felt as if she was in a horror movie, and if James hadn't been at her side, she knew for sure that there was no way she'd be there.

"We have to check the back. The lady said he was inside this building," James said.

"Well, I don't see him. All I see is a stack of clothes back here."

Suddenly, the clothing moved, and the gaunt face of Jesse turned to look up at her.

"Momma. Is that you?" he cried.

"Oh, dear God!" Alma exclaimed at the sight of his frail body.

As James lifted Jesse from the floor, something fell from his pocket and made a muted thud on the concrete ground. Alma bent down and picked up a mouthpiece for a trumpet. She followed James as he carried her son to the waiting taxi. Alma stroked his head as he lay on her lap, moaning softly.

"My poor baby. My poor, sweet baby."

chapter seventeen

Alma was surprised when James asked the cab driver to stop in front of his building. She had already made up her mind that she would not beg Dee to let Jesse stay with them. Alma knew of a motel up in Harlem she could afford until she found a treatment center that fit her budget.

"James, you really don't have to do this."

"What if I really want to?" he replied while handing her the keys to open his apartment. "I don't think you want to impose on Sister Dee any more than you probably feel you are. I have plenty of room, and it's a great excuse to keep you close to me."

"His skin looks so dry. I think he's dehydrated."

"I have a bottle of Gatorade in the fridge. Why don't you

pour him some, and I'll make you something to calm your nerves."

The sherry that James gave Alma took effect in just three sips. Warmth came over her as James closed the guest-bedroom door quietly behind him.

"He's sleeping now, but we need to find him a detox center before he makes up his mind that it will be too hard. Crack wasn't designed to let you quit by your own free will."

Alma got up enough courage to ask Dee humbly for her contact.

"Her name is Dr. Nadiv Winters. She runs the June Retreat in upstate New York. She said there was a bed available for Jesse. Forgive me for making the call without your permission, but I figured since you didn't hit me, you would be back to take me up on my offer," Dee said as she handed Alma the notepaper with the address and phone number.

"This place sounds expensive."

"It is, but Nadiv is a Red Hat and promised that you would be able to use your insurance."

"How am I going to be able to do that?"

"Alma, don't ask so many questions. Just take her up on the offer."

"I don't know how to thank you, Dee."

"You don't have to. It's what our sisterhood is all about."

Alma leaned down and kissed Dee on the cheek, thanking her.

James had rented a car to drive them upstate. Halfway there, Jesse woke up in the backseat, and he was angry.

"Where are you taking me? Stop this car, man. I've got to get back out there."

"Out there where, Jesse?" Alma asked. "I'm taking you to get some help."

Jesse attempted to open the door and jump out.

"I swear to God, if you jump out this car, boy, I will get behind that wheel and run you over myself. Now, for the last time, sit back and shut your mouth!" Alma yelled.

Jesse saw the venom in her eyes and closed the door. He feared her more than he did falling out of a speeding car. When they reached the June Retreat, Jesse was sleeping again. Two orderlies wheeled him inside on a gurney after Alma filled out the paperwork. Nadiv Winters was a pretty, plump East Indian woman with long black hair pulled back into a perfect bun on top of her head. Her reading glasses hung by a beautiful eighteen-karat-gold necklace that caught Alma's attention as they shook hands.

"I am happy to meet you," she said in a thick Indian accent. "Don't worry about Jesse at all. He will be fine. In a few weeks, you won't even recognize him. One thing you have to promise me, and I make everyone promise this, do not under any circumstance allow him to convince you that he is cured. It is an addict's con game to get out before the treatment is finished."

"Trust me, I'm not a pushover," Alma said cockily.

"The other thing that I ask is to make yourself available for some group-therapy sessions with him in the near future."

"Why do I need therapy?" Alma asked.

"A lot of times, the underlying causes for addiction stem from issues of resentment and anger fostered in childhood. We need to attack those issues in order to free him of his need to escape. That is the only cure to his addictions."

For the next few weeks, James was a great camp counselor for Alma. He could feel her inner turmoil as a concerned mother and was determined not to let her sink into the depression that beckoned her.

Every time the phone rang, Alma's heart dropped. Most times, it was Jesse begging for her to come get him.

"I'm cured, Momma. I don't need to be up here with all these white people. Most of them are alcoholics, anyway. They need the extra time to heal. I don't want to do crack anymore. It's out of my system. Please come get me."

"Dr. Winters told me that you must complete the entire six weeks. I promised her I wouldn't help you escape until she said you were cured, Jesse."

"I hate it here. These people are weird. They keep talking about God and sponsors. They get off the drugs and alcohol and get addicted to God and sponsors!" he cried.

"An addiction to God is a good thing, son. Turn your life over to him, and everything will work out fine."

"You turned your life over to him, and what did it get you, Momma? You're still just as mean and angry as you were when Daddy was alive," he shot back.

"I have to go, Jesse. I will not let you take your anger out on me!"

Alma's hands shook as she hung up the phone. Where had that come from? How could he be so disrespectful of his own mother? *I'll bet Kenny never said such hurtful things to Stacy. I'm ashamed to be his mother,* she thought.

"Are you all right?" James asked from the seat next to her in the movie theater.

"Yes."

"You need to turn the volume down on your thinking, Miss Alma. I can hear your thoughts over here," James joked. "I'll bet you don't even know what this movie is about."

"I'm sorry, baby. My head is somewhere else."

"Do you want to take a walk?"

"Yes."

"I've never been mad while walking," James said as they crossed the street and headed for their spot by the water.

"I love it down here." Alma sighed. "The water is so peaceful. Even though it's so dirty it looks like an oil spill, it still calms the soul."

"You calm my soul, Alma," James confessed, holding her from behind. He softly hummed "Trust in Me" into her ear.

Alma turned to face him. His eyes smiled with sincerity, and she could feel their hearts beating in perfect rhythm as they leaned against each other on the railing.

"Can I kiss you?" she asked.

James nodded as he gently pulled her toward his waiting lips. Their tongues danced slowly and both of them kept their eyes open, gazing at the lust reflected in the mirrors to their souls. The kiss was so passionate that another younger couple walking by actually stopped in their tracks and took pictures, admiring what they didn't believe was possible for older couples.

"We're causing a scene here," James commented.

"Good," she replied. This was a pleasant distraction for her. "I can do this all day."

"Me too."

"May I kiss you again?" she asked.

"Only if you promise to do it for an eternity."

"I can't promise you that."

"Of course you can," he said, dropping to one knee before her, with the young couple as witnesses.

"James, what are you doing?"

Looking down at him, she knew that this kind of perfect moment only happened in the movies. In fact, it had happened in the movie she just saw, but she hadn't been paying attention the way she was right now.

"Alma, I've only known you for several months, and yet I feel like I've known you a lifetime. Your kiss, touch, and smile are all I think about. I want to make love to you. I want to see you when I wake up and hold you when I go to sleep at night. I can't stand to be away from you. I love you, and most important, I respect you. If you would say yes to be my wife, I swear I will treat you like a queen, and I will make you the happiest woman in the world. Will you marry me?" He held open a jewelry box, revealing the most beautiful, elegant antique diamond engagement ring Alma had ever seen.

She looked over to the young woman, who had tears rolling down her cheeks. This was the proposal she had always dreamed about as a little girl.

"I don't know what to say."

"Say yes!" the young woman yelled as her camera flashed.

"Yes," Alma said through tears of her own.

Dee got up out of her wheelchair and hopped around on one foot in a celebratory jig for Alma, who was all smiles as she showed off her ring.

"I can't believe it! I swear, I need you to pinch me and tell me I'm not dreaming." Alma squealed with delight. "Ouch!" she said after Dee squeezed her arm hard. "I feel like the luckiest woman in the world."

"He's the lucky one, Alma. You have to let me tell the girls. I know how private you are, but you haven't seen unity until you see the Red Hats throw a wedding. How much money are we working with?"

"I don't know. James said that he wanted me to have fun with it. His only stipulation was not to bug him too much with the planning of it. He basically just wants to show up with the rings. Maybe we should wait until James gives me the budget first."

"Absolutely not. He said he wanted you to be his queen, right? Well, a queen has got to look like one on her wedding day. Besides, whatever he allows you, we will get it done for half of that. I know several travel agents who can get us fabulous deals on some beautiful resorts in Connecticut or Long Island by the shore. Oh, my God, I'm just as excited about this as you. How about the Bahamas for your honeymoon? There's a sister at the Paradise Cove who works in reservations and will get you the presidential suite for a regular suite price if it's not booked already," Dee said as she finally sat back in her wheelchair.

The girls all met up at Marie Callender's for tea. Alma made sure she sat next to Dee, just in case someone tried to slip her a piece of celebration pie. They all shrieked as Alma delivered the good news. Alma could tell that Joy was putting on a brave face as she embraced her to congratulate her.

"I'm happy for you, Alma. He is a great man, and I'm sure you two will be an amazing couple," Joy whispered.

"Thank you," Alma whispered back.

"When y'all finish all the hugging and kissing over there, I want to tell Alma about my friend Ann's dress shop. She has a wedding gown in the window that is something out of a storybook. Maybe I can talk her into letting you borrow it for a day," Magdalena said.

"I'm not borrowing my wedding dress. I'd rather not get married than have to hide tags while I say my I do's. That is so tacky!" Alma said.

"I was just throwing it out there."

"Well, I'm throwing it right back. Thank you, but no thank you. I never had a wedding before. I just showed up at the courthouse the first time around. I want to remember this one, because I don't plan on doing it again."

Stacy used one of her contacts in high society to book Alma the Montauk Yacht Club in East Hampton for a super discount as long as the wedding took place on a Sunday afternoon. The dress Alma fell in love with wasn't her size and would take ten weeks to deliver—it was an Italian design by Antonio Bertucci, who handmade every one of his creations. So the girls surprised her with a visit from a sister who was a costume designer for films and specialized in making knockoff gowns. Freda Minx was used to working under pressure and promised to have the dress fitted and made in five weeks for the cost of the fabric.

Alma was walking on air about the wedding, but a phone call from the June Retreat brought her back to the ground quickly.

"This is Dr. Winters. I'm calling to invite you to our first group-therapy session, this Saturday at nine o'clock. I suggest you get here a half hour earlier so we can have a brief discussion beforehand and I can lay out some guidelines to help you manage your emotions in the room."

"Why do I have to manage my emotions? This is about his addiction."

"It's about healing, Alma. Sometimes we have to dig deep to get to the root of his pain. I hope you bring an open heart and a calm mind, because that will speed up his recovery," Dr. Winters cautioned.

As soon as Alma hung up the phone, apprehension set in. Had she gotten the phone call a year ago, she would have let herself wallow in disappointment and fear. But she knew that as much as she dreaded being exposed to this stranger, opening herself up to others could bring blessings—like having a good man who reciprocated her love, having friends who wore red hats and purple dresses, and possibly having her son back. That was worth any emotional roller-coaster ride she had to endure.

chapter eighteen

"I felt like garbage my whole life. Do you have any idea what I had to go through, with all the neighborhood kids teasing me constantly about being a little bastard? I wanted to run away and die, but I was afraid that neither one of you would miss me," Jesse said through bitter tears.

Alma sat across from him with her eyes squinting as she relived her infidelity and the gross smell of Seymour's hot, liquored breath in her nostrils.

"My mother's a ho, my father was a coward . . . and I'm a crackhead! What did you expect me to be? This is what you get when you don't have parents who love you."

Fed up with his disrespect, Alma reached across the coffee table and slapped Jesse in the mouth.

"Do not talk to me like that again!" she screamed. "Don't you ever question my love for you, boy." Alma stood to pace. "Do you have any idea of the sacrifices we made for you? Who do you think changed your diapers? Took you to school? Bought your clothes? Nursed you when you were sick, ran your baths, made your meals, told you bedtime stories, and combed your nappy hair? That takes a love and commitment that only two loving parents can give. If you want to be mad at me, I will live with that, Jesse, but I will not let you talk bad about a man who is not here to defend himself. Harold loved you! And even though you've tested me beyond my limits, I still love you." She stormed out of the room.

Too angry and sad to cry and too hurt and numb to move, Alma stood in the corridor by the elevators, watching people exit the steel boxes. A young man still standing inside one held open the closing door for her.

"Miss, are you getting on?"

Alma didn't respond, so he let the door shut, muttering his disapproval of her silence. A moment later, Dr. Winters approached her from behind.

"I know it doesn't feel this way, but that was a major breakthrough for him. Jesse is angry with a lot of things. If you give him time, I'm sure he will get through the resentment and see that you were a loving and kind mother."

"I should have never come here."

"You have to come back inside, Alma."

"For what? He hates me. The best thing I can do for Jesse is to leave him alone."

James stood in his doorway, scratching his head with a perplexed look on his face as Alma shoved the engagement ring into his hand.

"I can't do this. I'm sorry," she said.

"Hold on, Alma. Come in here, and let's talk about this. After all, my life is affected by your decision, too." He gently reached for her hand and escorted her into his place.

Even in her irrational frame of mind, Alma subconsciously noticed that the large oil painting of his ex-wife was covered by a cloth on its perch above the fireplace.

"Now, tell me why the sudden change of heart."

"You don't want to marry me, James."

"Yes, I do."

"No, you don't. I'm not a good woman. I will hurt you."

"I don't believe that. I just think you are stressed out from the wedding planning. If you want me to help out with the arrangements, I'll roll up my sleeves and get involved."

"It's not that at all. I was having a ball planning the festivities. It would have been beautiful."

"You mean it *will* be beautiful. I'm not letting you go that easy, Alma. Now, I want you to exhale and just tell me what's on your mind. Maybe I can help you solve whatever is troubling your sweet heart."

"This heart of mine is not sweet. You have no clue what you're getting into, James!"

"Well, why don't you tell me everything you think I should know and then let *me* decide if I want or need to retreat? Just tell, don't edit," he warned.

James listened intently as Alma told him the dark things of her past. Everything about her and Harold, her pregnancy out of wedlock, the shame it brought upon her parents. The distance it caused in her relationship with her mother and how she never even tried to fix it. Her hatred for her father. She told James about Harold's infidelity and the years she spent trying to get revenge on him for sleeping with her best friend. How after her affair, she'd contemplated an abortion and how even after giving birth, she had a hard time accepting Jesse as her son, because he was a constant reminder of her sins. The immense guilt that burdened her every step, remembering all the years of hurtful things she used to say to her unfaithful husband in front of her innocent son. And that the fear of repeating the cycle of dysfunction with James was too much to bear. James held her hand and listened without judging or interrupting. When she finished her monologue, she waited for his response.

"So?"

"So, now I love you even more," he said. "The fact that you can articulate your past mistakes so well means you have given things a lot of thought and truly have regrets, which means you are determined not to repeat that course. Your problem has a simple solution. A painful one, but if you do it right, you can bring closure to many of these things that haunt you."

"What is the simple solution you're talking about?"

"Saying you're sorry to someone is different from letting someone feel that you are sorry. That takes prayerful meditation and a heartfelt conversation. Your son got caught in an emotional shoot-out. He didn't ask to be born into that situation, but he was. If I were Jesse, I'd want you to take responsibility for your actions and reassure me that you will rededicate yourself to being the mother I know you can be. Most men don't like to live in the past, but if they don't resolve those past issues, they can't see their future."

"I don't know, James. I still think we should put the wedding off."

"If we do that, what am I going to do with this?" He made his way over to the covered painting and removed the veil.

"Oh, my God in heaven," Alma whispered, seeing an oil painting of James on one knee proposing to her, with the sun setting in the background and the river's water reflecting the skyline. "It's beautiful," she said, hugging him tightly.

"That is the woman I see when I look at you. Lovable, vulnerable, and beautiful."

"I'm so scared. I don't know what to do."

"It's going to be OK. Trust me, everything will work out fine. I promise," he said, kissing her neck tenderly.

Alma rehearsed the speech in her head as she walked toward the June Retreat entrance. She turned to get a look of encouragement from James, who remained seated in the rented town car in the parking lot. He winked and blew a kiss. Alma shifted the package she carried into the other hand, then returned the gesture as the electric doors whooshed open in front of her. Dr. Winters was there to meet Alma at the reception desk.

"Don't worry, I will be right there if things get out of hand," Dr. Winters said.

"I need to do this alone."

"Are you sure?"

"He's my son, and I don't think it helps either of us to have a referee in the room."

"Last time you were here, you had serious reservations about confronting your fears. If you don't mind my asking, how will you overcome that?"

"He's my son. I'm simply going to speak to his heart, with mine."

Alma inhaled deeply, then exhaled slowly, as she eased open the door that led to the cave of confrontation. Jesse stood with his back to her, staring out the windows overlooking the gardens. His skin had returned to its normal color, and it was obvious that he'd finally gotten back to bathing regularly.

"Hello, son."

"Hey," he replied without turning to see her.

Alma set the package down on the couch next to her and waited for him to turn around. "Aren't you going to sit with me?"

"I'd rather stand. It's a better view out here," he said, stabbing her with his bitter tone.

"Jesse, I never meant to hurt you. What happened between your father—Harold and me wasn't about you. It was just two people not knowing how to communicate or love each other correctly."

"Humph," Jesse replied.

"OK, maybe it was about you—at least, it became about you. I was young and dumb, with no idea of how to manage my emotions. I was angry with Harold for making me cross the line of who I was or thought I was as a woman. I compromised my own morals and the value I placed on the institution of marriage by laying with Seymour—whom I hated—just to get back at the man I loved. I was wrong. I don't expect you to forgive me, son. I only pray that you'll try to understand me. People make mistakes, and the biggest mistake I made was not putting aside my anger. I saw how special you were as a baby. Do you know that you walked before Todd and Angel? Anything you wanted to do, you just did it, including playing that trumpet. I don't even know where you got that thing from."

"Seymour gave it to me."

"No wonder I hated it so much. Whatever happened to it?"

"I owed a guy some money, and he beat me up and took it."

"I'm sorry to hear that," she said.

"Not as sorry as I am."

Jesse turned to face his mother with the coldness of an enemy. His eyes squinted just as hers did when she disapproved of something or someone.

"Why are we talking about my trumpet?" he asked.

"I was walking around today, trying to figure out what I was going to say to you, and I just couldn't for the life of me find the right words. That's because there are no words that can erase the pain I caused you. I know that. I have to own that for the rest of my life. I actually stopped in the middle of the street with tears in my eyes and begged God to help me reach your heart. I said, 'Show me a sign, God.' And then something shiny caught my eye, and I turned to see this." She handed him the package off the couch.

"What is it?"

"Open it," she said. "It's a gesture."

Jesse hesitated, then took the shopping bag, lifted the red velvet satchel out of it, and opened the drawstring to reveal a brand-new trumpet. It was brushed gold in color, and the look on Jesse's face said it was special.

"Wow! This is a Zeus Olympus made by Dave Monette! Only the best of the best play one of these babies."

"Do you like it?" she asked.

"I love it."

Alma smiled and handed him the mouthpiece she had in a small custom-made box, which looked like a tiny coffin with a red silk lining. "Why don't you play something for me?"

"You hate the way I play."

"I never really heard you play. It would mean a lot to me if you did."

Jesse turned down his glare and slowly attached the mouthpiece to the horn. He stood by the window, with the sun shining behind him casting a backlight that gave him a silhouette. He played his heart out as Alma closed her eyes and swayed to his rendition of Miles Davis's "So What."

The music played softly as the guests stood at their seats on the lawn, facing the flowered gazebo overlooking the marina at the Montauk Yacht Club. It was a seventy-two-degree sunny day in spring when Alma glided down the aisle toward James, who wore a pale gray suit with black lapels that matched his shoes and belt. The tie was a darker shade of gray and sat nicely against his blush-pink shirt. A red pocket square matched the ones worn by the groomsmen lined up beside him. Alma wore a three-quarter-sleeved, empire-waisted, floor-length ivory wedding gown with a modest reverse neckline fastened with five large pearl-shaped buttons, lovingly done by Freda Minx, complete with a short-sweep train that moved fluidly with her every step. The look of a queen.

Through her matching lace and beaded veil, she kept eye contact with James as she clutched her bouquet of red roses and walked through a sea of Red Hats toward her future lover, husband, and best friend. They exchanged their vows before Todd, Angel, and Jesse through smiles and tears, confessing love and gratitude to God and each other for the happy times now and to come.

"Hear, hear," Dee said, tapping her champagne glass at the head of the reception table. "Today I witnessed what most little girls dream of from the time they are old enough to fantasize about finding their Prince Charming and riding off into the sunset to live happily ever after. I hope that dream comes true for Alma and James. I pray that you always keep a piece of this beautiful day with you, so that when times get difficult, you can look back and smile, remembering all the love that was shared today. May God bless you and your marriage through eternity." She raised her glass and sipped in unison with the family and guests.

"Thank you," Alma said, mouthing the words under the applause from across the table.

Alma lifted the window shade on the plane to peek out at the sun, which shone so brightly the heat warmed her face.

The champagne she sipped in her first-class seat eased her nerves. The bubbly had flowed from the moment she was seated. Suddenly, the 767 hit an air pocket. James instantly stuck his hand out for her. He gave Alma a reassuring smile as she grabbed hold of his strong hand. *This isn't so bad,* she thought.

Two hours later, they were checking into their presidential suite at the Paradise Cove. When the bellman opened the door, Alma saw red rose petals laid out on the floor leading to a magnificent super-king-sized bedroom with an ocean view, so close and beautiful you could taste the water as the waves crashed against the rocks below. James took a hot shower in the second bathroom as Alma enjoyed a bubble bath in the master suite. They nervously met between the sheets with only two chocolate strawberries as foreplay. They fed each other, then allowed their lust to be the dessert.

"I love you, Alma Debron."

Alma didn't know what she said in return, but it was loud enough to wake up the planet.

acknowledgments

Sue Ellen Cooper and the Red Hats, I salute you for being such a wonderful worldwide sisterhood. You have brought much joy to many lives. I've witnessed it firsthand, through my mother.

I want to thank the entire WAYANS CLAN (brothers, sisters, children, and grandchildren) for their love and support, especially my parents. Pops, I love you very much. You don't get thanked enough for the example you have set before your sons as a man of integrity and self-sacrifice. Momma, thank you for taking me back and forth to hospital after hospital to get my clubfoot fixed. I don't have any idea how you paid for it, but you saved me a life of pain and humiliation by getting it done at such an early age.

Aunt Muriel, thank you for always making me feel special as a little boy. It helped shape me as a man.

Aunt Moe, thank you for your love and kindness. I will never forget how you let me into your home as a young man. That was a wonderful time in my life. Uncle G, I love you and appreciate all the visits you and Aunt Trudy made to see me the hospital.

Shout out to all my cousins, again way too many to mention individually so I thank them all.

I send my love to the Wayans on my dad's side of the family. Thank you to Don Reo and Dean Lorey, my good friends who went before me paving the way with ink into the wonderful world of writing books.

Joey Vassallo, thank you for everything, my brother.

Bob Nedd, I see you!

I want to say thank you to my book agent, Lydia Wills, for helping get this novel published. Your excitement meant a lot to me as an author.

To Judith Curr and her incredible staff at Atria, I send my heartfelt gratitude for working with me on *Red Hats*.

Special thanks to Malaika Adero, you were a joy to work with as my editor. Your great notes and gentle prods helped get me through this.

I also want to thank Alysha Bullock, Todd Hunter, Donald Goble, and Jon Moonves.

If I've forgotten to mention anyone else who has helped me along the way, I'm sorry or . . . maybe I didn't on purpose. LOL.

—Damon